2.00

CHERRY AMES, MOUNTAINEER NURSE

The CHERRY AMES *Stories*

Cherry Ames, Student Nurse
Cherry Ames, Senior Nurse
Cherry Ames, Army Nurse
Cherry Ames, Chief Nurse
Cherry Ames, Flight Nurse
Cherry Ames, Veterans' Nurse
Cherry Ames, Private Duty Nurse
Cherry Ames, Visiting Nurse
Cherry Ames, Cruise Nurse
Cherry Ames at Spencer
Cherry Ames, Night Supervisor
Cherry Ames, Mountaineer Nurse
Cherry Ames, Clinic Nurse
Cherry Ames, Dude Ranch Nurse
Cherry Ames, Rest Home Nurse
Cherry Ames, Country Doctor's Nurse
Cherry Ames, Boarding School Nurse
Cherry Ames, Department Store Nurse
Cherry Ames, Camp Nurse
Cherry Ames at Hilton Hospital

☆ ☆ ☆

The VICKI BARR *Flight Stewardess Series*

Silver Wings for Vicki
Vicki Finds the Answer
The Hidden Valley Mystery
The Secret of Magnolia Manor
The Clue of the Broken Blossom
Behind the White Veil
The Mystery at Hartwood House
Peril Over the Airport
The Mystery of the Vanishing Lady
The Search for the Missing Twin
The Ghost at the Waterfall
The Clue of the Gold Coin

"Bruce's granny hates me an' all my folks," Eliza sobbed.

Cherry Ames, Mountaineer Nurse

CHERRY AMES MOUNTAINEER NURSE

By

JULIE TATHAM

NEW YORK

GROSSET & DUNLAP

Publishers

COPYRIGHT, 1951, BY
GROSSET & DUNLAP, INC.

ALL RIGHTS RESERVED

PRINTED IN THE UNITED STATES OF AMERICA

Contents

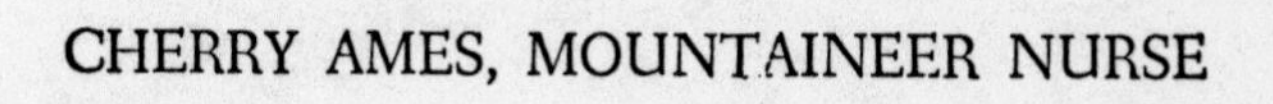

CHERRY AMES, MOUNTAINEER NURSE

CHAPTER I

Heartbreak Hollow

NOW THAT THE APRIL SUN HAD SLID DOWN BEHIND THE rocky ridges, it was cold in the valley. Cherry hurried along, hoping Bertha would have set a match to the blazing logs in the fireplace of their small room behind the makeshift clinic.

Cherry was as tired as she had ever been in her whole nursing career, but she knew that plump Bertha Larsen, who had been hobbling around on crutches all day, would be even more exhausted. Cherry glanced up at the sunset, veiled by the mist that hung above the thickly wooded mountain. Lonely little cabins perched precariously on the lower slopes of it; gray, unpainted barns dotted the hillsides. Between the pastures and the farm lands narrow dirt lanes spiraled, following the path of mountain streams.

In the growing twilight, Cherry felt hemmed in by the dark-green palisades. There was something almost sinister about the shadows that lay across the valley floor. Desolate Mountain had certainly been well named. Cherry felt sure that there could not be another village in the whole state of Kentucky as isolated as Heartbreak Hollow.

But in spite of the fact that the people were poor and, for the most part, ignorant, it was a happy place. Daniel Boone, it was said, had given the village its name, because, after an attack by the Indians, only two of the original frontier families had survived. Later, other pioneers had come to build their log cabins and to struggle for existence side by side with the Smiths and the Clarkes. They brought with them the customs, idioms, and traditions of their English, Scottish, and Irish ancestors, and even now the older members of the community were reluctant to relinquish them.

The children, in spite of their sporadic schooling, were slowly but surely freeing themselves of the idioms and superstitions. In general, the fathers, although they kept saying they didn't want to be "beholden" to the doctor and the nurse, were much more modern-minded than the mothers. But the grandparents were not of the twentieth century and didn't want to be.

Their attitude made it difficult for Cherry in her work. Although the women obeyed their husbands implicitly, they were really ruled by two old midwife grannies, Mrs. Deborah Clarke and Mrs. Martha Smith. They regarded with suspicion preventive and curative medicine. In fact, Granny Clarke regarded Cherry

Ames herself with suspicion for she had only been with them for three days. She had not yet met Granny Smith and felt sure that the old woman had purposely stayed in her room the day Cherry had called with Dr. Jessup. Bertha, who had been working in the hollow for several months, said that Granny Smith was slightly older than Granny Clarke, who looked as though an April breeze might blow her away. But whenever they were needed they trotted for miles over rough roads up and down hills without showing any signs of fatigue.

Cherry opened the door of the clinic and stood for a minute staring disconsolately at the clean wooden shelves, pathetically bare when they should have been filled with much-needed supplies. Dr. Jessup had promised to bring more whooping cough serum on his next weekly visit by helicopter. Cherry couldn't help wondering if next Saturday might not be too late.

She knew that the incubation period was from one to two weeks, and that the infection was usually transmitted during those two weeks before the "whooping" began. Until then, it was very difficult to diagnose. Of course, Billy Carter's slight fever and violent coughing attacks might mean that he had nothing more than a spring cold. But Dr. Jessup had left instructions with Cherry that if Billy emitted the characteristic "whoop," or vomited after coughing, he was to be isolated until one week after the last symptom.

"That," he had told her with his reassuring smile, "is easier said than done. About the only thing you can try to do is prevent him from coming in contact with the very young and the very old. As you know, ninety-five per cent of the deaths occur in kids under five, and it might be fatal for Granny Clarke, who can't seem to remember whether she had the 'chin cough' as a child or not."

The Clarkes lived about a quarter of a mile down the hill from the Carters, and considered themselves next-door neighbors. And Granny Clarke had been sitting on Billy's bed that morning and again that afternoon, frowning at Cherry when she took his temperature.

"Hi," Bertha called from the other room. "Are you going to stay out there all night, Cherry?"

Cherry hurried through the chilly clinic into the warmth of the nurses' quarters where a fire was blazing.

"You're a wonder," she told Bertha as she toasted her cold, tired fingers. "I can't seem to get used to springtime in the mountains. It's warm all day, then suddenly when the sun goes down it's freezing. I didn't dare hope you'd have a fire waiting for me."

Bertha was sitting on one of the two huge beds that took up most of the space in the small room. She was resting her injured foot on a rickety cane-bottomed chair. "It's you who are a wonder, Cherry Ames," she said, her china-blue eyes twinkling. "*I* didn't dare hope you'd stay more than one day in this forsaken spot. When you hopped out of Frank Jessup's helicopter I was never so glad to see anyone in my life. And then when Granny Clarke snapped at you, I was afraid you'd fly back to Titusville that evening with Frank."

Cherry sniffed. "You weren't afraid of anything of the kind, Bertha Larsen. I love it here. It has charm and beauty and the people are fascinating. If you'll let me borrow your camera I'd like to take some pictures to send home." She took her writing case from a cupboard. "Which reminds me. I've got to write Mother now while I have the time. All she knows is that you had an accident and sent for me." She handed Bertha writing paper and a fountain pen. "And *you* have got to write Mai Lee. If only you could send along some samples, too."

"But, Cherry," Bertha protested, "Mr. Spofford, who is a dyed-in-the-wool New Yorker, said you were all wet when you told Eliza her granny's hooked rugs would sell for thirty or forty dollars on Madison Avenue."

"That man's no judge." Cherry wrinkled up her pert nose. "He and his perfumed hair pomade. Ugh! If he had any taste he'd know that there's no smell quite as nice as *no* smell."

Bertha chuckled. "You certainly took an instantaneous dislike to our handsome 'city feller.' "

"Oh, I suppose he means well," Cherry said. "But I don't think he should encourage the Clarkes and the Smiths to sell that land. They were all set to plant tobacco until he arrived with his offer of five dollars an acre."

"A hundred dollars," Bertha pointed out quietly, "is a lot of money to these people. And they'd donate most of it to the clinic. Josh Clarke helped pay for the baby scales, you know, and Lincoln Smith gave Frank the money for the adult ones."

"I know," Cherry argued, "but unless I'm way off in my prices, they could raise enough money on the lovely things in the community loom house to build a small hospital. Those hand-woven blankets and ties and scarfs are really exquisite."

"You may have something there," Bertha said. "If Mai Lee can find just the right shop, it'll certainly pay much more for Granny Smith's beautiful blankets than the measly five dollars she gets from that store in Titusville."

Cherry nodded. "Even if they all together can't sell their handicrafts for enough to build a small hospital, I'm sure they can raise enough money to pay a teacher another thousand dollars a year. With an increase in salary one of them might be willing to stay throughout the term, instead of quitting as soon as winter sets in."

"You're right," Bertha agreed. "But even though the kids' parents would do almost anything in order to keep a teacher here from July through February, I don't think—"

"Oh, Bertha," Cherry interrupted impulsively, "we simply can't let the mule train take those lovely things to Titusville Wednesday morning. You've got to do something about it. These people love and trust you;

I'm still a 'brought-on' woman. You're the only one who might be able to persuade them."

"I'll do the best I can," Bertha said doubtfully. "I'm pretty sure I can get permission to send Mai Lee some samples, but I'll never be able to talk them into keeping all that stuff here until the mule train comes back next month. They worked all winter at their looms, Cherry, and they need the money so desperately!"

"I know," Cherry admitted, "but a month's delay might mean the difference between thousands of dollars and a few hundred." She sighed. "Well, do the best you can anyway. And when you write Mai Lee, give her my love and tell her that if she wants to, she can sublet my room at No. 9. She knows some gals who are living in a dreary hotel at the moment and who would give their eyeteeth to get out of it even if it's only for a few weeks."

Cherry curled up in front the fire, thinking about the cheerful Greenwich Village apartment which she and five other graduates of Spencer Hospital's training school had shared when they were visiting nurses. Mai Lee, the lovely Chinese-American girl, was the only one on duty in New York now. Gwen and Josie were taking postgraduate courses in another city, and Vivian Warren was in South America with her husband. The last reunion of the Spencer Club had been at her wedding in December, but Bertha had not been able to come.

She had sent Vivian a handsome hooked rug and had written No. 9, "Since the November rains have washed away all the roads, the only way to get in and out of here is by helicopter. But I can't leave, anyway, because Santa Claus is bringing five families new babies for Christmas."

Bertha had met young Dr. Jessup while he was a resident at a New York hospital. He had told her about Heartbreak Hollow and how he planned to return to his home in Titusville soon, and would pay the isolated little community weekly visits by helicopter. "Even the Frontier Nursing Service hasn't yet reached that section of the mountains," he told Bertha. "I just happened to be flying over the hollow one day and landed out of curiosity. Since then I've never been able to rid my conscience of the plight of those landlocked people. If only I could be able to find an R.N. who would be willing to live there all the year round!"

Kindhearted Bertha had promptly volunteered, and a few months later he had sent for her.

"I admire Frank Jessup," Bertha wrote in December, "more than any other doctor I've ever worked with. Outside of his practice in Titusville he has a small income from stocks which he inherited from his grandfather, and I suspect he spends most of it on Heartbreak Hollow. The people here are proud but desperately poor. Those who can, insist upon paying him, but he won't accept anything except farm produce; chickens, hams, eggs, vegetables, and such. They can't seem to understand that my salary is paid by the county, and are always trying to give me presents so they won't be 'beholden' to me. I've finally compromised by letting them take turns giving me all my meals except breakfast, which I fix myself in a very rustic way over a log fire.

"Because they are paid such pitifully low salaries, no teacher will stay very long, and none at all will come during the months when the roads are impassable—November through March. The children are all starving for education. The schoolhouse is just one big room with greased-paper windowpanes, but it is kept scrupulously clean and painted, and the men keep the woodbox filled to the brim. The nearest high school is on the other side of Desolate Mountain, a day's journey away by horse or mule. So is the nearest doctor. This sounds as though he was a mule, and he is, in a way. On the rare occasions when he has been sent for, he has flatly refused to come, saying that he is too busy with his own patients, which is probably true.

"Before Frank Jessup discovered the hollow's plight, the only medical care they had was at the hands of two midwife grannies, who, because of a feud, have never spoken to each other since their weddings years and years ago. Granny Clarke's great-granddaughter, Eliza, and Granny Smith's great-grandson, Bruce, are courting, finally with the approval of their parents. It was Frank who made Lincoln Smith and Josh Clarke realize that they had no right to let their great-grandfathers' quarrel ruin their children's lives.

"The Smiths and the Clarkes are now very friendly, with the exception of the grannies, who apparently will not break their wedding-day vows. They are both furious because Bruce and Eliza plan to get married in April when the mule train brings in supplies again for the first time since the November rains. It's what you might call a portable general store and carries everything from calico by the yard to very precious glass for windowpanes; also the mail, if any. It's an old family tradition of the Clarkes' that no girl can get married without a new pair of shoes. The people here only buy their children shoes once a year, usually when the mule train arrives around Halloween on its last visit. Eliza will have an extra pair this year, a momentous event in itself!

"I know you're all dying to hear more about the feud. It started way back when the grannies were little girls. The Smiths and the Clarkes, the two oldest families, own the only really fertile land in the hollow. Their homes are built high up on hills and face each other. In between is a huge rolling field that belongs to both families. No one has set foot in that field since the feud began. Eliza's great-great-grandfather, Lazarus Clarke, and Dolph Smith, Bruce's great-great-grandfather, each had four husky sons. At that time the field was divided into two sections, and one year the families decided to pool their manpower and plant the whole field with tobacco. They all worked hard and raised a bumper crop the very first year. When Lazarus took it to the market he came back with the astounding sum of ten thousand dollars.

"Of course this could easily have been divided equally between the ten men, but so much money soon started arguments. Jeremiah Smith said that Gabriel Clarke hadn't worked half as hard as he had. Ezekiel Clarke, who had nine 'young'uns,' said he should have at least twice as much as Clabe Smith, who had only four. The two youngest sons (who eventually married the grannies) were dismissed by both families as mere 'shirt-tailed lads' who should be content with enough 'pay money' to buy some 'decent duds.' Things went from bad to worse and the 'rifle guns' were got out. During the shooting a fire started which burned away most of the Clarkes' woodland. When the smoke cleared, only the two youngest sons were still alive, and they called a truce. The money would be equally divided between them and they would go on working the land together. But then it turned out that Lazarus had apparently died before he could tell any of his sons where he had hidden the money. This infuriated young Elijah Smith, who accused young Clarke of lying. Clarke was so insulted that he swore he would never speak to a Smith again. Elijah not only swore that he would never again speak to a Clarke, but vowed that until the money was produced he'd shoot anyone who set foot in the tobacco field. Smith, in his turn, said that *he* would shoot anyone who set foot in the field, and to this day not even children have been allowed to play there.

"Granny Clarke claims that she and her husband searched every inch of their home and the land around it, but never found the money. She is convinced, as is everyone else except Granny Smith, that Lazarus hid it in a hollow tree and that it was destroyed during the fire. Granny Smith thinks differently. She stubbornly insists that Debby Pettit Clarke got the money from her husband, who always knew where it was hidden, and has been hoarding it ever since. I thought she was going to have a stroke when she heard Bruce was courting Eliza, and I very much doubt if either granny will attend the wedding.

"Anyway," Bertha had written in conclusion, "that is the story behind the hooked rug I sent Vivi for a wedding present. Granny Clarke painfully made it with her own arthritic little hands. I talked her into selling it to me instead of sending it to the Titusville store with her other rugs when the mule train arrives in the spring. I can't believe that anyone who works as hard as she does with her swollen fingers is hoarding a small fortune, can you?"

Cherry, remembering the letter Bertha had written to No. 9 in December, couldn't believe it either. She had seen Granny Clarke's disfigured joints and knew that soon the little old lady would not be able to use her hands at all. She turned to look up at Bertha.

"You don't believe that magic spring water has any real medicinal value, do you? Why, Granny Clarke has been drinking 'yallerroot biled down' in it for years, and she has a bad case of arthritis. Who is this philanthropist who is supposed to have sent Mr. Spofford here to buy the land around the spring?"

Bertha shrugged. "I don't remember that Mr. Spofford mentioned the name of the man he is representing. All I know is that some rich New York gentleman, a victim of arthritis himself, plans to build a sanitarium here so that arthritic cripples can benefit from the spring water. As to its medicinal value, Cherry, I don't know what to say. All the people in this valley swear by it. And you have to admit that Granny Clarke is the only one afflicted with arthritis, which, in her case, is nothing but a degenerative disease."

"That's true," Cherry admitted. "And I suppose the only way to prove whether or not the spring has any effect on arthritis is to try it over a period of time on a group of patients."

Bertha nodded. "And the only way that can be done is for someone to build a sanitarium here. And the logical place to build it, since the spring is in the Clarkes' woods, would be in the old tobacco field."

"Well," Cherry said, "the whole thing sounds fishy to me. How did the philanthropist hear about the spring in the first place?"

"Oh, the driver of the mule train or one of the teachers," Bertha said calmly, "probably told someone who told someone else."

Cherry sniffed. "It's a long distance between here and New York. I don't trust that Spofford man, Bertha, and I hope the Smiths and Clarkes won't sell their land to him for a measly hundred dollars. Why, if they planted tobacco now they might raise another bumper crop!"

"They might," Bertha agreed, "and ten thousand dollars would certainly solve most of Heartbreak Hollow's problems. But growing tobacco is a tricky business, Cherry. It there's a drought this summer, or worse, too much rain, the crop wouldn't amount to a row of pins." She smiled down at Cherry's flushed face. "Cheer up, honey. If Eliza and Bruce hadn't brought the feud to an end, I think their families would have sold that land. After all, lying idle like that, it wasn't worth a cent. But now that they're speaking to each other for the first time in their lives, I feel sure Linc and Josh, with Bruce and Malcolm's help, will want to try for another bumper crop."

"I hope so," Cherry said, and began the letter to her mother. "I know, darling," she wrote, "that the hasty wire I sent you last week must have been baffling. Especially the 'letter follows immediately' part. I forgot in the hectic rush of answering Bertha's hurry call that the only way to get mail out of here is when the mule train comes once a month, or via our flying doctor on Saturdays. I didn't have time to write you before he flew back last Saturday. I hardly had time to breathe that first day. What with Bertha herself being a patient and five babies all under four months old, most of whose mothers had never even heard of vitamins until Dr. Jessup—but I'd better begin at the beginning!

"A week ago Saturday when, lucky for Bertha, Dr. Jessup was here, she tripped on a loose floor board on one of the porches and tumbled down the steps, badly spraining her ankle. He strapped it, but because the ligaments were so badly torn, he wants her to stay off it as much as possible for the next three weeks. She has been hobbling around on crutches which Josh Clarke made for her, but that's dangerous because there aren't any paved sidewalks here or macadam roads.

"Bertha was in despair because, as I told you when I was home Christmas, she was the only nurse Dr. Jessup could find, after trying for months, who was willing to stay in this inaccessible little hollow. She knew that Mai Lee and I were the only members of the Spencer Club who might be free to come and help out, so she wrote us both air-mail letters. Dr. Jessup, who doesn't have morning office hours on Mondays in Titusville, spent the weekend here, as he sometimes does in emergencies. So I didn't get my letter until Wednesday. My last patient, that nice Mrs. Jensen I wrote you about, was discharged from the hospital that morning, but she insisted that I spend the first day home with her. It was almost eleven o'clock when I got back to No. 9. I read Bertha's letter, a note from Mai Lee saying that she couldn't leave her patient, sent you a wire, another to Dr. Jessup, and after many frantic calls to the airlines, finally boarded a plane at LaGuardia Field. The flight to Louisville was thrilling, but not half as exciting as flying over these Kentucky mountains in a helicopter.

"We started out so early in the morning that the sun hadn't yet burned off the fog which rose up from the valleys in the shape of huge ghosts. No wonder people here are so superstitious! After a while I could see the rivers, lined with willows and winding between hills that are pink and white with dogwood and redwood blossoms. When I fly back, Dr. Jessup says they will be ablaze with rhododendron.

"Below us were beautiful four-lane roads arching rivers and cutting right through mountains. Dr. Jessup said that Heartbreak Hollow is undoubtedly the only community in Kentucky that is not connected to the main highways by the rural-mail and school-bus routes. Just on the other side of towering Desolate Mountain is a thriving town which is as modern as Hilton.

"We hovered above Heartbreak Hollow for a bird's-eye view, and I could see the men, women, and children working in the fields, plowing, spading, and planting. Even the six-year-olds, of which there are ten who have never been to school, help with the farm work. Now that there's no school because there isn't any teacher, the children of all ages work from dawn to dark. They go barefoot because they've outgrown the shoes their parents bought them last fall, and are all as healthy as can be, except for one who Dr. Jessup suspects is coming down with whooping cough. I hope not, because Billy Carter, like all the people here, loves babies. And up until Saturday when we ordered him to bed, I suspect he may have paid visits to all five of them. Although they are still a little young, they could, of course, be given whooping cough shots, but their parents wouldn't hear of it. They can't abide the sight of a hypodermic syringe, and the grannies are convinced that being 'jabbed by the needle' is as bad as being bitten by a copperhead. Only the children who have already attended school have been inoculated against diphtheria and whooping cough. Dr. Jessup insisted that, before he would let them all crowd into one room, they must be given the all-in-one whooping cough, diphtheria, and tetanus shots. I'm terrified for fear there may be an epidemic among the six-year-olds which might spread and be fatal to the babies. They should, of course, be isolated for the next three weeks to be on the safe side, but how are we going to make their parents understand that they must not be hugged and kissed by the six-year-olds, who may even now be in the early, infectious stage?

"We landed in a pasture, and the ewes and baby lambs have grown so used to the flying doctor's visits that they 'paid us no mind.' But the people from all the near-by farms rushed up to meet us. Bertha waved a crutch at us from the porch of the clinic, which is nothing but a two-room log cabin. Dr. Jessup got the men to build it last summer and bought most of the supplies with his own money. It's really more of a first-aid station than a clinic, with a very rustic kitchen table on which the patients are examined. Water has to be brought in from the well in front, and instruments are sterilized on a little alcohol stove.

"Dr. Jessup was very much pleased when Bertha told him that I had only recently given up my night supervisor job. 'Your experience,' he said, as we started off to see Billy, 'will come in very handy here. In between my visits you'll have to make decisions which you wouldn't be faced with anywhere else.' It made me sort of nervous. Bertha is so much more calm, cool, and collected than I ever will be!

"But Dr. Jessup is so reassuring and so good-looking. Tell our harum-scarum young neighbor, Midge, that she would fall in love with him on sight. He's as tall and blond as my twin Charlie, and has a wonderful smile that lights up his whole face. I think it's his smile, almost as much as his professional skill, which makes the people here admire and trust him. Even the very old men and women respect him, and the children idolize him. Unlike most of their parents, they have no fear of the shots.

"Dr. Jessup called a meeting in the community loom house before he left, and talked with the parents of all children who are not immune to whooping cough. Smiling, but speaking in a very serious voice, he reminded them that the older kids had survived their vaccinations and shots. Then Mrs. Bella Smith, who lost three children in a whooping cough epidemic several years ago, spoke up and said, 'The doctor-man is right. Every young'un should hev the needle.'

"There were many amazed whispers at this because she is Granny Smith's granddaughter-in-law, and Granny Smith, I hear, is a tyrant. Dr. Jessup felt that young Mrs. Smith's little speech had a very good effect on the others.

"Bertha and I are not the only 'fotched-on' folks.

There's a man from New York who arrived on horseback late Saturday evening. He says he's here representing a rich man who plans to build a big sanitarium near the magic spring. The water is supposed to be a cure-all.

"Mother, I wish you could hear these people talk! Their dialect has the rhythm of poetry. They drop their g's and prefix a's so that the words sort of lilt along together. They say Aprille instead of April, and it describes this lovely month much better than anything I could ever say with my Illinois twang.

"I'm too tired to write any more, darling. After you and Dad and Dr. Joe and his imp Midge have read this letter, will you pass it on to Charlie? I'll never have time to write him at such length, but I'd certainly love to get a long letter from him. Please, all of you write me soon, care of Dr. Frank Jessup, Titusville, Kentucky."

Just then someone tapped on the clinic door, and Cherry hurried into the other room. Waiting on the porch with a napkin-covered basket on her arm was a young girl, who, Cherry saw at a glance, had been crying. Her wavy, molasses-colored hair had been tossed by the evening breeze, and one small hand clutched a shawl that was sliding off her thin shoulders.

"Hello, Eliza," Cherry greeted her. "You've brought us our dinner and look frozen. Come right in and get warm by our fire."

"Hit don't matter, Miss Cherry," Eliza Clarke said in a sad little voice. "Nothen matters no more." Her round blue eyes were filled with tears.

"What on earth has happened?" Cherry asked in alarm. "Is someone sick at your house?"

Eliza shook her head. "Jist me, Miss Cherry, an' I'm heartsick, that's all. Bruce, he's not speaken to me." She handed the basket to Cherry and turned away, burying her face in the crook of her arm.

For a moment Cherry was so surprised that she could do nothing but stand there, limply holding the supper basket. Bruce Smith was not speaking to Eliza Clarke! Did that mean the old feud had flared up again?

CHAPTER II

Evening Visitors

ELIZA'S TEARS, CHERRY QUICKLY DECIDED, MUST BE THE result of a lovers' quarrel. The feud *couldn't* have flared up! Why, only that afternoon the four men had put the finishing touches to the little cabin that would be Bruce and Eliza's new home. Panes of glass for its windows would arrive tomorrow on the mule train, and so would Eliza's new shoes. The wedding was scheduled to take place as soon as the "singen-preacher" arrived.

"You're chilled to the bone, honey," Cherry said gently. "Come inside and get warmed by our fire before you take that long walk back up the hill to your home."

"I cain't, Miss Cherry," Eliza sobbed. "Maw's a-waiten fer me. I've been gone quite a spell. I waited and waited at the spring fer Bruce, jist as I allus do, 'cause sence Bertha hurt her ankle bone he's been holpen me carry the supper basket to her." She raised her head then and proudly squared her thin shoulders. "I waited there ontil it was 'most dark an' then I seed him a-comen down the lane, walken fast. I called out to him that the corn bread would be cold if we didn't hurry, an' he kept a-comen, an' he walked right past me, Miss Cherry, sayen ary a word, not even looken at me, standen there a-holden out the basket to him."

Cherry impulsively gathered the taut little body in her arms. "Never mind, darling," she crooned. "You must have said something to hurt Bruce's feelings without realizing it. But he'll get over it. Don't forget, he's going to help you pick out your wedding shoes when the mule train comes tomorrow."

Eliza pulled herself free. "I never said anythen to hurt Bruce's feelens. It's that granny of his. She's set him agin me. She hates me an' all my folks." With that, she jumped off the porch and raced away into the shadowy woods.

Cherry stared after her, not knowing quite what to do. She was, she knew, still a "brought-on" woman to these people. The very fact that Eliza had confided as much as she had was a compliment. The Clarkes and the Smiths, although polite and very hospitable, usually maintained an attitude of suspicious reserve with "furriners." Cherry realized that it would be hopeless for her to try to patch up a lovers' quarrel between Bruce and Eliza.

Bertha, whom they had all learned to love as one of their own, would have much better luck. She couldn't, of course, hobble through the woods and up the hills to either home, but every member of both families would surely be waiting in front of the loom house tomorrow evening when the mule train arrived. Perhaps Bertha could do something then to bring the young people together.

But when Cherry suggested the idea to her over supper, Bertha sadly shook her head. "I've been afraid of this," she said. "Those two old grannies are as stubborn as mules. They are both bound and determined to keep those kids from getting married."

"They're not really kids," Cherry protested. "If they had attended school regularly, Eliza would be graduating from high school now and Bruce, from college. They are certainly old enough not to let an ancient feud ruin their lives."

Bertha shrugged her plump shoulders. "You don't know these people, Cherry. The family is the core of the community; united they stand, divided they fall. Granny Smith probably laid down the law to Bruce at the last minute, knowing that when Eliza's shoes arrive tomorrow, there will be no excuse for postponing the wedding."

"But still," Cherry argued, "Bruce had no business walking right by Eliza like that without speaking. The least he could have done was to explain to her that he couldn't marry her without his great-grandmother's consent."

"That *does* surprise me," Bertha admitted. "Something must have happened which we know nothing about and probably never will know. I can hardly believe that Eliza told you as much as she did. I doubt if she would have told me as much. You must have done something pretty remarkable to win her confidence so quickly."

Cherry thought for a minute. "I didn't do anything remarkable, Bertha, but you know how Eliza adores her twelve-year-old sister, Lucretza?"

Bertha nodded. "She worships the ground that little redheaded tomboy walks on. If it were the other way around—Eliza not speaking to Bruce—I'd suspect that Lu had something to do with it."

"I would, too," Cherry said. "And for some reason, which I can't fathom, Lu has a crush on me. Instead of planting lettuce as her mother told her to, she insisted upon following me around all morning. I suppose she's like a lot of other twelve-year-olds who form violent attachments for their teachers."

"That's right," Bertha said. "Lu is the big-red-apple type. She was wild about the last teacher we had, who did look a lot like you. Slim and pretty, with lots of curly brown hair. Miss Scope stayed from July through October and seemed to love it here. I was surprised when she told me at the Halloween party that she wasn't coming back this spring."

"Lu told me all about Miss Scope," Cherry said, with a laugh. "In fact, she tried to tell me everything about everybody in the hollow. I wouldn't listen to her gossip, of course, and finally made her go home. But I suppose her attachment for me has influenced her big sister. Otherwise, Eliza probably would have handed me the supper basket without saying a word."

"That's the answer," Bertha said. "Love me, love my Lu is Eliza Clarke's motto. And if anyone knows why Bruce isn't speaking to Eliza, it's Lucretza Clarke. Young as she is, if we had a newspaper that little scamp would write the gossip column."

"Speaking of writing," Cherry said, suddenly changing the subject, "I've an idea which I've been dying to discuss with you all day."

"Oh, no," Bertha moaned. "I hope it doesn't mean I'll have to write another letter. That lengthy epistle I scribbled to Mai Lee left me exhausted."

Cherry laughed. "It involves you, but you won't have to do much writing. All you'll have to do is supervise other people's writin' and readin' *and* 'rithmetic."

Bertha glared at her suspiciously. "Cherry Ames, are you trying to make a schoolmarm out of me? You know I was born and bred on a farm and ain't got no larnin'." She sighed. "But I know what you're driving at and I've been thinking the same thing way down deep inside me for the past week. While I'm laid up like this, there's no reason why I couldn't run sort of study hall for the younger children, the ones who are ready for the three R's."

"I knew you'd do it," Cherry cried excitedly. "Only, instead of a study hall, my idea is that you'd run a boarding school."

Bertha reached for her crutches. "I'm getting out of here," she said, giggling. "You've lost your mind."

"No, I haven't," Cherry said soberly. "Sit back, Bertha, and listen, please. I'm almost positive now that Billy Carter has whooping cough. When I stopped in late this afternoon, he had a violent attack, and ended by vomiting. I begged his mother to let me start him on chloromycetin capsules, but, of course, with Granny Clarke glowering at me, she refused."

"Cheer up," Bertha said. "When he starts whooping, she'll give in. You and Frank both told Mrs. Carter on Saturday that taking four chloromycetin capsules a day usually means that the vomiting and whooping stops after the fourth day."

"We certainly *tried* to explain the wonder drug to her," Cherry said. "But what worries me is that all the kids should have had the three-in-one shots before they were a year old. And since he's been playing with the other six- and-seven-year-olds during the most infectious stage, I'm afraid there'll be an epidemic in that age group. Which, unless we isolate the children who are not immune and have been exposed, will spread to the babies."

"So that," Bertha interrupted, grinning her approval, "is what you meant by a boarding school! An isolation ward with me in charge?" She frowned. "If none of the kids develop any symptoms during the next three weeks, they can go back home. But if even one of them shows signs of a cold, the boarding school might run all summer!"

Cherry nodded. "Whether they all come down at once, or one at a time, or not at all, you'll have to have help. That's why I wanted you to tell Mai Lee to rent my room at No. 9. I won't leave if there's an epidemic. And I'm sure that girls like Eliza and her chum, Kate Pettit, will be glad to give as much time as they can to such a community project."

"Their mothers, too," Bertha agreed. "We'll have a Parent-Nurses Association meeting tomorrow in the loom house while everyone will be there waiting for the mule train. It's a wonderful idea, Cherry, and we won't have any trouble at all getting an unanimous vote of approval. The schoolhouse is the logical place. The men can move the desks to an empty barn and bring each child's cot from home. I can sleep comfortably on a bed half the size of this one myself, fat as I am. Sure you won't mind staying here alone at night?"

"You did before I came," Cherry reminded her, smiling. "If one of Granny Smith's witches should bother me, I can always move over to the schoolhouse with you." She sobered. "No, the only thing that worries me is that some of the parents may object because they need their kids to work on the farms."

"Objection overruled," Bertha said cheerfully. "In the first place, all the parents are very anxious for their children to receive as much education as possible. In the second place, there's a nice plot of land behind the schoolhouse which can be plowed up in one morning. The kids can do their own planting, hoeing, and weeding, and they'll love eating what they've grown themselves from start to finish. Someone, I'm sure, will donate a cow. Little Jenny Pettit is an expert milker. The Wrangels will give us some chickens; they've got more hens than they really need. My idea is that we'll be completely independent; in fact, we'll undoubtedly grow more vegetables than we need, and they can be put up in jars for hot school lunches next fall. That is, if we have a teacher."

"Well," Cherry said, thrilled that Bertha thought her plan would work out so well, "you're teacher as of now. I'm leaving the whole project in your capable hands."

Bertha grinned. "Take your own capable hands out to the well and bring in some water. I'll wash the dishes."

"No, you won't," Cherry told her firmly. "It's time schoolmarms like you hobbled into bed. You've got a big day ahead of you tomorrow." She picked up the bucket and went out through the clinic to the yard.

The mist above the mountaintops had cleared and the rising moon was shining brightly in a black velvet sky. A shadow moved out of the woods beyond the well.

A man's voice said, "Hello there, Miss Ames. I was just going to call on you two young ladies. I'm delighted I arrived in time to be of some help." It was Mr. Chase Spofford, Cherry knew. The perfume of his hair pomade permeated the night air. He came closer and took the bucket from her unwilling hands. "Here, let me fill this for you."

"Don't bother," she said coolly; then realizing that she was being rude, added, "Thanks a lot. I'm so tired, I wasn't sure I could work that old pulley." After all, she had no real reason for her instinctive dislike of this man. He had a perfect right to slick down his black hair with anything he liked. If only the scent were not quite so strong.

When he came back with the water she said, trying not to wrinkle up her nose, "You're very kind. I'm sorry I can't ask you in for a cup of coffee, but Miss Larsen has already gone to bed."

"I'm disappointed." He set the bucket down on the porch. "I wanted to talk to you about little Eliza Clarke. I'm staying there now, you know."

"I didn't know," Cherry said. "I thought you were the Carters' guest."

He smiled. "Well, with the little boy whooping up his meals, I thought I might be inconveniencing them. So I threw myself on the mercy of the Clarkes, who very hospitably gave me their spare room."

"They're very hospitable people," Cherry said. "Everyone here is. Why did you want to talk to me about Eliza?"

The smile faded into a puzzled frown. "Why, just this. When she left to bring you your supper she was the gayest young lady I ever had the pleasure of knowing. When she came back she looked like one of her granny's ghosts. She ate no supper and didn't say a word throughout the meal. I was wondering if perhaps you knew what caused her change of mood."

"I'm glad you told me she isn't looking well," Cherry said evasively as she picked up the bucket. "She did seem chilled to the bone when she was here. I begged her to come in and get warm, but she said her mother was waiting for her. I do hope she isn't catching a cold with her wedding date so near. I'll look in on her tomorrow and take her temperature." She turned the knob of the clinic door and said over one shoulder, "Many thanks again. Good night."

"Good night," he said pleasantly. "You might take old Mrs. Clarke's temperature tomorrow, too. In my opinion, she's delirious."

Cherry almost dropped the bucket as she turned around to face him. "Oh, my goodness, I'll go right over there. A high temperature in a woman of her age can be very serious." Then she saw that he was laughing.

"I'm sorry I upset you," he said, his eyes mocking. "I was just joking. There's nothing wrong with Mrs. Clarke except senility. She swears she saw the devil sneaking out of the barn early this morning." In an exaggerated hillbilly tone of voice he mimicked, " 'The devil's aimen to fotch me off fer sure,' she told me when I tried to make her relieve the pain in her hands with the aspirin tablets and hot-water bag you left there this morning. 'Them pilts hain't a-goen to do me no good now,' she argued. 'I seed Satan hisself, with his long red tail, a-traipsen out o' the barn.' "

"She told me the same thing when I met her at the Carters' this afternoon," Cherry said. "I tried to explain to her that pain often distorts one's vision. What she saw, of course, was fog in one of the grotesque shapes it often takes in the early morning."

She left him then with a rather curt good night and went in to repeat the conversation to Bertha. "The very idea," she said indignantly, "of that man keeping me out there all that time just because he wanted to gossip!"

"He's fallen for your charms," Bertha said, with a teasing smile. "All men do. You should be used to it by now."

Cherry hung the water bucket on the hook above the blazing logs. "If he's got any sense he'll soon realize that I don't like him. Even if I did, I wouldn't sit around in the evening while he makes fun of my patients. When *we* try to imitate their dialect we do it because we're fascinated by the poetry of their language. But when he talks about them there's the most condescending expression on his face which I find very annoying."

Bertha yawned. "I don't think you're being quite fair, Cherry. You said yourself that he seemed genuinely worried about Eliza."

"I know I did," Cherry admitted, "but after thinking it over, I think the truth of the matter is that he was just plain curious. He's one of those nosy people who like to pry into other people's secrets. He probably guessed from the way Eliza looked at the supper table that she had quarreled with Bruce and came over here hoping for all the details. There is nothing," she said emphatically, "so despicable as a male gossip, unless it's one who perfumes his hair."

"Oh, my stars," Bertha said, convulsed with laughter. "You've worked yourself into a real hate for that poor man." Suddenly she stopped laughing and held up her hand for silence. Then she pointed to the one small window. With her mouth she formed the words soundlessly. "Someone's—eavesdropping."

Cherry had heard the same stealthy sound too. She rigidly crouched by the fire, wishing for the first time since Dr. Jessup had flown her into Heartbreak Hollow that she had bolted the clinic door.

It was Bertha who broke the silence. Raising herself up on one elbow she demanded in a loud, clear voice, "Who's out there?"

At the same moment someone knocked loudly on the clinic door, opened it, and shouted, "Bertha, Bertha! It's me, Bruce Smith. Granny's taken on somethen awful. Could I kindly come in?"

"Of course," Bertha shouted back as Cherry sprang into life and opened the door between the two rooms. The tall, too-thin young man held a lantern in his hand, but even in that flickering light Cherry could see that his face was pale and drawn. His breath was coming in short gasps and she guessed that he must have run all of the way from the Smith farm to the clinic.

"Miss Cherry," he gasped, "Granny, she cain't seem to breathe. She's shorely a-dyen, an' hit's all my fault."

Bertha joined them then, hobbling and talking at the same time. "Calm down, Bruce," she said. "Your great-grandmother's not going to die. She's as sturdy as an oak. It's nothing but an asthma attack. If she'd only take her medicine when she feels one coming on—"

"No, Bertha," he interrupted. "Not asthma this hyar time. She's bad scairt, that's what. She heerd someone out in the old tobacco field a-diggen—a-diggen her grave, she says."

CHAPTER III

The Feud Flares Up

CHERRY DARTED BACK INTO THE BEDROOM, SLIPPED into her coat, and snatched up her satchel. Granny Smith was an old, old lady, suffering from bronchial asthma. If only she would take the medicine Dr. Jessup had prescribed, ephedrine sulphate with an anti-histaminic! And now the old woman had obviously been badly frightened. She might need adrenalin, but Cherry could not give her an injection without a doctor's orders, even if the granny would submit to the "needle."

"A-diggen her grave," Bruce was telling Bertha. "She's shore hit's the devil a-comen to fotch her. I didn't see nothen, Bertha, an' I don't hardly believe in the devil, but who could-a been diggen out in that field with the moon not yit up over the top o' Old Desolate? Ary a soul has set foot on that land sence my great-great-grandpappy's time!"

Cherry led the way out to the porch. "Then she heard

the disturbing sounds about an hour ago?" she asked. "What took you so long, Bruce?"

"I didn't come right off, Miss Cherry," he said. "Granny didn't say nothen about hearen things fer a spell. She jist set there by the window, a-staren an' a-listenen like she allus does when the witches talk to her. But I come fer holp soon as I seed she wasn't breathen right an' looked mighty ailen."

"Did she take her medicine?" Cherry asked worriedly, as they hurried along the path through the woods.

"Maw got hit out o' the cupboard," Bruce said. "An' was a-pleaden with her to take a mouthful when I tuck off. Reckon she's had a swaller by now."

"She'll be all right," Cherry said soothingly. "The sounds she heard were probably the wind blowing the treetops against the barn. And the person she thought was Satan must have been Mr. Chase Spofford. He came down here from the Clarkes' a little while ago and probably took the short cut across the field not knowing that he was trespassing on your property."

Gradually Bruce began to recover from his own fright. "Hit's like this, Miss Cherry," he confided. "I feel mighty guilty. Granny never wanted me to court Eliza. But I did. I couldn't seem to holp myself. I loved the purty leetle thing from the time I fust set eyes on her. She was sitten thar in school, right acrost the aisle from me, with her pigtails a-hangen down her back, all shiny an' smooth like 'lasses candy. I never tole Maw an'

Paw, but I reckon they knowed hit all along. Las' Christmas they said iffen I wanted to marry Eliza Clarke, I could; an' her folks the same. 'Cepten fer the grannies. My granny, she said all along that iffen I didn't stop a-goen with a Clarke the devil would come an' cause us a peck o' trouble."

"But you haven't had any trouble," Cherry pointed out quietly. "In fact, your two families may make a lot of money if you plant the tobacco field together."

"We hain't a-goen to plant hit," Bruce said mournfully. "Not sence Josh an' Malcolm Clarke done what they did."

"What on earth did they do?" Cherry asked in amazement.

"Spiled our wool," he told her sadly. "We had hit all ready to wagon down to the loom house so hit could go off on the mule train tomorrer. I was aimen to buy windows fer Eliza's house with my share o' the pay money. But when Paw an' I come up from the cornfield about sundown, thar hit was, all over the barn floor, mixed up with hay an' manure. Granny takes one look an' says Satan has been at hit with his pitchfork. Hit's a curse on us fer me courten with a Clarke." He sighed. "Afore we even righted up the barn, Paw makes me promise never to speak to a Clarke agin."

They had reached the footlog across the little creek that was fed by the spring now, and Cherry stopped, so choked up with sympathy she could hardly speak. "Bruce," she finally got out, "you know perfectly well the devil didn't ruin your wool. You must somehow make your father understand that it was done by human hands."

He helped her across to the other side and said, "I tried an' tried, Miss Cherry, but the onliest thing he said was that iffen it wasn't the devil hisself, then it must o' been Josh Clarke, Eliza's pa. No one else in this valley has ever held a grudge against my folks."

She started ahead of him up the rocky path to the Smiths' big, rambling, one-story house. It and the Clarkes' old, but lovely stone house were the only homes that boasted glass windows. The lamplight from within gleamed against the scrubbed-clean panes, and Cherry wondered if she would arrive too late. Fuel for light was a precious commodity in Heartbreak Hollow; the kerosene lanterns were only used in dire emergencies. If anyone wanted to stay up after supper, he had to be content with the light from a log fire. With an almost full moon riding high in the sky, Bruce had extinguished his lantern as soon as they emerged from the woods. Lamplight against the Smiths' windowpanes could only mean that someone was seriously ill.

The old gate creaked as Cherry pushed her way into the yard and hurried up the steps. A hound bayed from somewhere behind the house, and Cherry shivered in spite of herself. Bruce held open the door from the porch and Cherry stepped into the big, barnlike living room. In one corner stood a huge loom and in the other three were spinning wheels. There were two enormous stone fireplaces, rising from floor to ceiling, and crouched before one of them was old Granny Smith. She looked up as Cherry started across the room, and patted the clean, white kerchief she wore tied around her head.

She flashed a toothless smile of greeting to Cherry, but there was a baleful gleam in her faded eyes as she darted them disdainfully in Bruce's direction.

"Welcome," she said to Cherry in a quavering, high-pitched voice. "Light an' hitch up a cheer. I 'lowed as how you'd take a notion one o' these days to come a-callen on me."

Her grandson and his wife, Bruce's parents, appeared then from a sofa in the shadow of the loom. They greeted Cherry warmly, not as though she were a nurse, but as a guest.

"Oh, dear," Cherry thought as she sat in a chair beside the old granny. "They're furious with Bruce for running off to get me. I don't suppose the frail little thing will even let me take her pulse." Aloud she asked, "How are you feeling, Mrs. Smith?"

"Fair to middlin'," the old woman said. "A while back I was plumb tuckered out from weaven, an' that shirt-tailed lad thar, he got scairt. Unbeknownst to me, he took out fer Bertha. Bertha, she's got sense; stayed at home the way a body should atter sundown."

Cherry's cheeks flamed. She couldn't help feeling like a fool. Granny Smith obviously was no longer in need of medical attention.

"I'm sorry to have intruded at this late hour," Cherry

said humbly. "But I did want to meet you, Mrs. Smith. Bertha has told me about the beautiful things you weave, and everyone has told me what a wonderful nurse you are."

The old woman leaned closer to inspect Cherry's face. "My," she cackled, "hain't you the rosy-jawed lady! Niver did see the like. Why, you're the color o' them strawberry neckerchers I sold the city feller t'other day. Neckties, he called 'em, but I don't hold with sech talk. He paid me plumb proper fer 'em, so I let him tote 'em off, 'stid of senden 'em off on the mule train tomorrer."

"I'm sure he paid you much more than the Titusville store would have paid," Cherry said quietly.

"I bin weaven all my life," the old woman told Cherry proudly. "I cain't shear the sheep no more, nor wash an' kyard the wool, but I can spin an' dye hit. Red's my favrit color, an' in my jedgment you're as purty as the blossoms on a redbud tree. What might your name be, gal?"

"Cherry."

This brought forth a loud cackle of laughter. "Your mammy shore knowed what she was a-doen when she give you that un!" Mrs. Smith reached out and laid a clawlike little hand on Cherry's knee. "Now, honey, you take your foot in your hand an' go 'long home with you. You'll lose them rosy cheeks iffen you don't git proper rest."

Cherry took this opportunity to touch her fingers lightly to the old lady's pulse. It was strong and steady.

She stood up as the granny suspiciously withdrew her hand. "I've loved meeting you, Mrs. Smith. May I come see you again sometime?"

"Shore an' hit'd be a pure delight, Cherry," the old woman said heartily. "Heerd you was brought on by the doctor-man, like Bertha, who's a mighty knowen woman."

"Yes, I'm a nurse, too," Cherry said.

This brought forth another cackle of laughter. "Law, chile, I bin nursin' so long I cain't recall jist when I cotched the first baby. You come to me when you git in trouble."

"I will," Cherry promised meekly. "Thank you very much." She said good night to Bella and Lincoln Smith, and with Bruce by her side started down the rocky path to the creek.

"Granny shore took to you," he said in an awed tone of voice. "And she don't take to many folks right off. That city feller now, she don't like him nohow. I was that surprised when she sold him them matching neckties. He come around to see if Paw wouldn't sell him a passel o' land nigh the spring. Paw said he'd have to speak to Granny, but Mr. Spofford didn't git nowhere a-talken to *her*."

"She's right," Cherry cried impulsively. "I hope you won't sell any of your land, Bruce." To herself she added: "That man admired Granny Smith's neckties just to get on the good side of her. But he didn't fool her for one minute. She only sold them to him because he paid her more than she would get in Titusville."

Then it suddenly occurred to Cherry that Granny Smith might prove an ally when Bertha tried to persuade the other weavers to delay shipment of their handicrafts for another month.

Bertha was asleep when Cherry tiptoed into the room behind the clinic, so she waited until morning to relate the events of the night before. When she had finished, Bertha said, "I wasn't really too worried about Granny Smith. When she gets those asthma attacks she doses herself with her own garlic-and-onion syrup until she finally gets to the point when she has to relent and take ephedrine sulphate. She usually recovers with remarkable rapidity, but up until then is convinced that she's dying."

"Then you don't think she saw someone in the old tobacco field last night?" Cherry asked. "I figured that her devil must have been Mr. Spofford, who probably doesn't know that it's taboo."

"He knows it's taboo all right," Bertha said, sipping the coffee Cherry had brewed over the flaming logs. "And he knows the whole history of the feud. No, Granny Smith cooked up her devil as an excuse to keep Bruce's mother from urging Frank's prescription on her. Bella Smith is a very intelligent woman. I'm sure she knows that it wasn't the devil or a Clarke who spoiled their wool."

"Who do you suppose did?" Cherry asked.

"Wild dogs, maybe," Bertha said. "It's a shame, because now Granny Smith will never allow Bruce to marry Eliza."

Cherry lifted soft-boiled eggs from the kettle of hot water on the hearth. "Those two grannies are certainly matriarchs," she said. "Do you think Granny Smith might help you persuade the other weavers to delay shipment until we hear from Mai Lee?"

"We have a chance if she's on our side," Bertha said. "Martha Smith is not only a matriarch in her own home; she and Granny Clarke are held in awe by the whole community."

"I'm in awe of Granny Smith myself," Cherry said, with a laugh. "All the time I was there I felt like an awkward child in the presence of a *grande dame*."

Bertha's china-blue eyes twinkled mischievously. "And that was what made the little old lady, as they say down here, 'As happy as a 'possum in a 'simmon tree with the dogs a mile away.' She dotes on the meek and humble, and if the truth be known, she doesn't dote on me. When I first came here I didn't have sense enough to treat her like a *grande dame*. I was very firm with her when she refused to take her medicine. She had all the symptoms of cardiac asthma—at least from where I sat across the room. She wouldn't let me come any nearer, and when she finally did take her medicine, it was from young Mrs. Smith."

Cherry smiled. "She called you a 'mighty knowen woman.' "

"Pure sarcasm," Bertha retorted. "If anyone can lure her over to our side in the Mai Lee project, it's you, Cherry Ames."

"All right," Cherry said. "I'll try. You have enough to do today, anyway. I'll stop in to see her at lunchtime. She's too hospitable to refuse me an audience over corn pone and pork chops."

Cherry picked up her satchel and the empty supper basket and started off on her rounds. Fortunately, there were not any really sick people in the hollow. Billy Carter's temperature had never gone above 101. She hoped to arrive at his home before Granny Clarke and that if he was worse today his mother would let her give him his first capsule of chloromycetin.

Cherry's main job was to encourage the mothers of the five babies to follow Dr. Jessup's instructions. And that, she reflected, was quite a job. Before Dr. Jessup flew in on his first visit, babies "jist growed." And there were far too many tombstones in the hillside graveyard testifying to the fact that they didn't always grow up.

If a baby seemed hungry he was sometimes given a bit of corn bread, sweetened with molasses, and as often as not, a piece of fat pork to suck on. When he developed colic as a result, one of the two grannies was called in. Then the unhappy child was dosed with worm medicines, vile-tasting concoctions which did have the desired effect of emptying the patient's little stomach, but usually left him so weak and nauseated that he could not swallow his mother's milk. His fretful cries of hunger and misery were diagnosed by the midwives as the "teething sickness" which could only be cured by a dip in the spring at midnight when the moon was full.

When this ceremony was performed during the summer, the little victim generally survived, to go through the whole procedure over again until he became so toughened that he could digest almost anything. But the infant who was dipped on a bitter winter night almost always developed pneumonia. Then he was subjected to a treatment even more rigorous than the worming. To be on the safe side he was again dosed with a mixture of wormseed, sulphur, and molasses. Whether he kept this down or not, feverweed tea was forced upon him. This was brewed from bitter-tasting herbs; black seneca, goldenseal, yellowroot, feverweed, sweet fennel, ratbane, everlasting, and horsemint. Simultaneously with the dosing was the fever-breaking treatment. The scrawny little body was wrapped in a warm flannel cloth, which had been dipped in a mixture of coal oil, turpentine, and melted lard, and he was toasted on the granny's knees in front of the fire until he either survived or succumbed.

All this Dr. Frank Jessup had told Cherry on Saturday. "Your job," he had said, flashing her his warm smile, "will be to consolidate Bertha's and my gains. Bertha has made great strides—that girl is an exceptionally competent nurse—and her farm background has given her an instinctive and sympathetic understanding of these people. But unfortunately, her very competence, plus her success, has aroused the grannies' jealousies. Bertha delivered three of the Christmas babies herself. They were born in the middle of the week when I was not here. I myself have no fight with the grannies, and they accept me as a 'mighty knowen doctor-man.' I always ask one of them to assist at deliveries, and they really can be very helpful. But they resent Bertha because she is so young. And they will resent you too, for the same reason, plus the fact that you are exceptionally pretty."

Cherry had blushed although she knew Dr. Jessup was not paying her a compliment; he was merely telling her what she was up against. She had said humbly, "Maybe they won't resent me as much as they do Bertha. She's much more competent than I am. I always seem to get into scrapes wherever I go."

He had laughed. "No one in the medical profession could avoid getting into a scrape here. No matter what you do, someone is bound to criticize you, so don't let it worry you. Just do the best you can. I have come to the conclusion that our primary function here is to educate the mothers of young children. Each one eventually will graduate informally from a course in the home care of the sick. We can only accomplish this by the 'proof-of-the-pudding' method. For example, Baby Powell's mother has followed our instructions from his birth.

Compared to him, the other infants are puny. Of course, you can account for this partially by the fact that Lucy Powell had the best prenatal care that anyone in this valley has ever had. On each visit I gave every one of those five women iron tablets and capsules of dicalcium phosphate compound with viosterol. The other four, I have no doubt, fed their supply to the pigs, but Lucy religiously swallowed them down. She also followed my instructions for diet and exercise. In the beginning her blood pressure was as high as her blood count was low. By the end of the fourth month she was healthier than she had ever been, and still is."

"But why," Cherry had asked, "did Lucy Powell alone obey your orders?"

"Because," he explained, "the infant mortality rate on both sides of Baby Powell's family has always been appallingly high. Lucy's mother lost six of her nine children before they were a year old, and her mother-in-law's record was almost as bad. I'll never forget the day that Lucy came to me and said in a very frightened voice, 'I'm a-pinen for a young'un, doctor, but I'm a-feerd.' I soon assured her that she had nothing to fear. Now that she has an extraordinarily healthy child she is so grateful she can't stop singing my praises. If she sings loud enough, the others may hear and listen."

Remembering her talk with Dr. Jessup that first day, Cherry couldn't help worrying about Baby Powell, who was, indeed, the proof of the pudding. But whooping cough could break down the health of even a thriving infant, and the aftereffects could be very severe. In more ways than one it was important that Bertha's isolation ward be set up as soon as possible.

The sun was pinking the sky above the palisades now, and the air was fragrant with the flower-scented dew. The buds on the peach, quince, and apple trees were just about to burst into bloom. Cherry sniffed the rich, exciting odor of the plowed fields and listened to the sound of sheep bells and the crying of baby lambs in the pastures.

"Gee, haw!" It was Lucretza Clarke, shouting to her mule as it dragged the plow through the moist earth. The redheaded child looked too small for such work, but Cherry could see that her furrows were straight and the mule fully under control. On another farm the whole family was out planting corn. They had probably had their breakfast of sausages and gravy-biscuits in the pale light of dawn. There were no alarm clocks in Heartbreak Hollow; they were not, as Granny Clarke said, "needessary." For almost every family had at least one "crowin' rooster."

The hens were laying now and Cherry was glad because it meant coddled eggs for the babies. It was hard to convince some of their mothers that eggs were more easily digested than pork, and the babies themselves sided with their mothers.

Cherry hurried by the Clarkes' cornfield without calling a greeting to Lu. The impetuous child might well abandon her plowing for her latest crush. Young Mrs.

Clarke was out in front of the big stone house boiling clothes in a huge copper kettle. When she caught sight of Cherry she wiped her hands on her apron and came down the lane to meet her halfway.

"Mornen, Miss Cherry," she called. "I 'low you're on your way to see little Billy Carter next door. He's mighty ailen, he is. Cain't keep a thing on his stommick. Coughed all the night long, too. I didn't hardly close my eyes a-listenen."

"Did he whoop?" Cherry asked without much hope.

Mrs. Clarke nodded emphatically. " 'Long about dawn, he did. The same whoopen Eliza an' Lu did when they had hit. But they weren't hardly sick a-tall. Whooped an' coughed for nigh on to two months, but ary o' grain o' trouble they gave me. We was planten corn then, I ricollect, an' I let 'em rest in the shade when they had a real bad spell."

Cherry sighed. Mrs. Clarke was certainly not going to encourage any of the other mothers to have their children inoculated. "How is Eliza today?" she asked. "I'm awfully afraid she got chilled last night bringing us our supper. I hope she didn't catch cold."

A mask fell over the woman's face. She took the basket from Cherry and turned away. "Don't you go a-worren about Eliza," she said. "Git on to Carters' where your doctoren is needed."

There was nothing for Cherry to do but continue on up the lane. As she neared the spacious house that sprawled along the side of the hill, she could hear unmistakable sounds of whooping cough. In the yard, intermingling unconcernedly, were ducks, turkeys, chickens, pigs and a cow. The fowl skittered away, cackling, as Cherry approached, but the pigs kept right on rooting in the mud. The cow gazed at Cherry with uncurious eyes, then lowered her head to drink from the trough.

Cherry stopped to catch her breath after the steep climb and stared at the house. It had originally been a one-room cabin, and the other rooms had been added on as the family grew. Now that all the older children had married and gone to homes of their own there were rooms to spare; so on the rare occasions when Heartbreak Hollow had visitors they were always told that they would be "mighty welcome at Carters'." Here, Bertha had told Cherry, Jeremiah, the wandering minstrel, would stay on his annual April visit later that month. Cherry hoped that little Billy would be well by then. Bertha said that young and old loved to listen to the "ballats" Jeremiah sang to the accompaniment of the hollow's orchestra which included a banjo, fiddle, mandolin, guitar, and accordion. Cherry was looking forward to the wandering minstrel's visit almost as much as she was to the arrival of the mule train.

But right now the most important thing was to convince Mrs. Carter that Billy should start taking chloromycetin tablets. The door was open, so Cherry called from the crazily sloping porch, "Good morning, Mrs. Carter. May I come in?"

The boy himself answered, "Hi, Miss Cherry. I bin

pinen to see you. I got whoopen cough, I have, an'—"

His mother's voice interrupted, cross and hoarse from lack of sleep. She came out of the bedroom as she said, "Now, don't git him riled up with no talk o' needles, Miss Cherry. He's bad sick."

"May I see him?" Cherry asked, still standing on the porch. "I'm not going to give him a needle."

The woman immediately smiled. "Now, I declare, ain't I the uncivil one, though? I'm that tahd I've lost my manners, that's what. Come in, Miss Cherry, an' welcome. Billy, he's bin a-cryen fer you ever sence the cock crowed."

Cherry followed her into the other room. "Hello, Billy," she said, slowly moving toward the bed. "So you have whooping cough for me this nice, sunny morning?"

"I shore have," he said proudly. "An' I ain't aimen to turn black in the face. Gimme one o' them doctoren pilts, Miss Cherry. Don't pay Maw no mind. She's scairt, but I hain't."

"Good for you, Billy." Cherry sat on the bed. "I've got four little capsules in my bag. I want your mother to give you one now with a glass of water. If you take four a day every day until Dr. Jessup comes again, you'll soon stop whooping."

To Cherry's surprise and delight, Mrs. Carter immediately left the room and came right back with a glass of water. In another minute, Billy had had his first capsule, and was smiling happily. Cherry recorded his TPR on one of the patient's record blanks she always carried in her satchel.

Then she led his mother into the living room and explained that the basin must be disinfected every time Billy used it. "He should be given a little something to eat," she added, "a short while after he vomits. Eggs beaten up in milk and sweetened with honey would be the best thing for him. The medicine, you know, isn't magic. Billy won't get well right away, but by the time Dr. Jessup sees him again he should be all over the whooping stage."

The tired-looking woman nodded. "I should o' done like my Zeke said an' let the doctor-man give him the needle three weeks gone. Iffen I had, he might niver have done no whoopen."

"Well, there's nothing to worry about," Cherry said cheerfully. "If you keep him quiet and warmly clothed, he'll be well soon. But for the next few weeks he can't play with any children. Granny Clarke may want to come over and help you care for him, but you mustn't let her. Eliza and Lu can come because they have already had whooping cough. And so may any of your married daughters who have had it. But their children must stay away. Granny Smith, Dr. Jessup told me, had it when she was a little girl. So she can come. I'm going to see her today. Would you like me to ask her to pay you a visit?"

The woman smiled gratefully. "I hardly think my gals can lend me a hand. Sally an' Sue each got a passel o' young'uns, an' Pansy, she's got a suckin' chile. She's scairt to come nigh this house."

Cherry nodded. "Young Mrs. White is right to be afraid. Billy is a big boy going on seven. We won't worry about him. But we don't want Pansy's baby or any of the other babies to catch it from him."

Just then Eliza Clarke called from the bottom of the lane. "Mrs. Carter, oh, Mrs. Carter! Granny's a-comen to holp you nurse Bill jist as soon as she kin. Said to tell you she'd stay the night, too."

"She cain't," Mrs. Carter shouted back. "She might cotch it. Thank her very kindly, but say I'm a-gitten Granny Smith."

"Oh, oh," Cherry thought as she hurried down the lane. "That's not going to pour oil on the troubled waters." "Eliza," she called, "may I see you a minute? Wait, please."

The young girl met Cherry at the bypath that led to the spring. Before Cherry could catch her breath, she said, "If you feel to, I could go 'long with you this mornen an' holp you with the least'uns. Maw said I could. I kin bathe 'em real good now, sence Bertha larned me."

"I know," Cherry said. "And I'd love to have your help. The babies should be bathed every day unless they have colds or are ill, but most of their mothers are so busy they can't."

As they passed the Clarke house, the granny came out on the porch. "Mornen, Miss Cherry," she said coldly.

"Heerd what Mrs. Carter hollered to Eliza, I did. What kind o' outlandish nonsense was that? I ain't a-goen to cotch nothen from Billy. I bin a-doctoren chilluns most o' my life, an' ary cotched a thing." She pulled her bent body erect. " 'Pears to me like you is a-gitten above your raisen."

Cherry bit her lip. "I'm awfully sorry, Mrs. Clarke. I didn't mean to be bossy. It's just that Dr. Jessup left orders with me which I have to follow. He said that if Billy did have whooping cough, you were one of the people who mustn't go near him, because you didn't have it when you were a little girl, like Granny Smith did."

At the magic phrase "Dr. Jessup," the angry glint faded from the old woman's eyes. Cherry went on hastily, "He knew you'd want to help Mrs. Carter take care of Billy. He said you were a wonderful nurse, so wonderful that he didn't want to take any chances on you getting sick. This is what he said to me just before he left on Saturday, 'Take good care of Granny Clarke. I couldn't get along without her.' "

The old woman chuckled, smugly patting her kerchief. "I'll 'low he didn't say nothen like that about Marthy Smith. Iffen Billy ain't bad sick, she kin nurse him. I'll take keer o' myself like the doctor-man said." She turned and shook a gnarled finger under Eliza's nose. "Mind now, chile. Iffen you should meet up with a Smith while you're a-holpen Miss Cherry, you're to pass him by jist like he wan't thar. Hear?"

"Yes, ma'am," Eliza said dutifully, her round eyes dim with suppressed tears.

"Should you take a mind to smile at Bruce," the old woman warned, "I'll make your paw beat you half to death. Them Smiths," she snapped. "Them varmints." She turned back to Cherry. "Knowed what they did to us las' night? Pizened the hog we was a-fatten. Pizened him dead, they did."

"Oh, no," Cherry gasped. "They didn't. They—they couldn't do such a dreadful thing. It must have been an accident. I mean, the hog must have got hold of some poisoned fox bait."

"Ain't no sech thing," the granny retorted. "We got a passel o' hound-dogs to take keer o' foxes. Hound-dogs didn't bark when Bruce come a-sneaken up to our hog-pen las' night. Didn't bark 'cause they knowed him. That," she finished with an angry glance at Eliza, "that's what comes o' courten a Smith." She went back into the house and slammed the door.

Cherry stared speechlessly at Eliza, who was blinking back her tears. There could be no doubt now that the feud had started up again. Had Bruce, under orders from the Smith matriarch, really poisoned the Clarkes' hog?

CHAPTER IV

Cherry Wins a Victory

AS THEY STARTED ALONG THE BYPATH THAT LED TO Baby Powell's home, Cherry said to Eliza, "Honey, don't feel too badly. Things will work out; I know they will. It's a terrible misunderstanding between the two families. Did you know that yesterday someone went into the Smiths' barn and ruined the wool they were going to send off on the mule train?"

Eliza nodded. "Lu, she told me that. But my pappy didn't do it, Miss Cherry. Nor did my brother, Malcolm. Why, Malcolm, he's jist about the gentlest man hereabouts."

"I know," Cherry said. "I know no one in your family would play such a mean trick on anyone. And I'm also sure nobody in the Smith family poisoned your hog."

"Then who did, Miss Cherry?" Eliza asked tearfully. " 'Tain't no one else in this hyar valley who holds a grudge against my folks. The onliest ones is the Smiths."

"Well, Bruce didn't do it," Cherry said in the most reassuring voice she could muster.

"Bruce, he wouldn't want to," Eliza agreed. "But his granny could make him do 'most anythen she had a mind to. He's terrible a-feerd of her jist like I'm a-feerd of my granny."

"They're both wonderful little old ladies," Cherry said thoughtfully. "It's too bad that feud has always kept them enemies. Otherwise, they'd probably be the best of friends." Suddenly she stopped. "That's what we've got to do, Eliza. Somehow, we've got to make them break those vows they made so many years ago. If they'd only say just one word to each other, then the spell would be broken. After that, they'd probably have plenty to say, and the mystery of who's playing these cruel tricks on your families would quickly be cleared up."

Eliza shook her head sorrowfully. "The onliest way to make them break their wedden day vows is fer someone to on-airth that lost money, Miss Cherry. And that just cain't be done. All o' my great-great-grandpappy's offsprings done sarched for hit. Hit hain't nowheres on our land. Hit was most likely burned up when Granny was a young'un."

Cherry sighed. "I'm going to drop in on the Smiths around lunchtime," she said, "hoping they'll ask me to eat with them. They will, of course, because they're as hospitable as your family. If you'll let me, I'd like to tell them what happened to your hog. I'm sure Bruce will find a way to let me know his family had nothing to do with the poisoning."

Hope glimmered in Eliza's round blue eyes. "An' you kin tell his folks we didn't dirty up their wool?"

Cherry sighed again. "I can only tell them that I'm almost certain neither your father nor your brother would do such a thing. But I'm afraid that, unless we find out who did, nothing I can say will make any difference." They followed the blue waters of the stream down a slope to the Powells' trim log cabin.

In Cherry's opinion, this home was the loveliest in the whole hollow. It nestled among dogwood and red bud trees, and neat flagstone walks led from the house to the barn and the shed. There were already tiny green seedlings in the vegetable patch, and a neat barbed-wire fence enclosed the chicken run. The cow and her calf were grazing in a field on the other side of a fieldstone wall. Beyond the pasture was the orchard, and budding blackberry bushes grew along the wall.

Mrs. Lucy Powell, her plump baby in her arms, waved to Cherry from the sunny porch. "He's a-doen fine, Miss Cherry," she called. "No reason fer you to stop here this mornen."

So Cherry and Eliza smiled and waved and hurried on to the next house. Mrs. Carter's son-in-law and daughter, Pansy, lived here with their tiny baby. Little Jonathan White, Cherry felt, was too tiny. Even allowing for his small-boned frame, he was underweight, and this should not be attributed to the fact that he was cutting his first tooth. Dr. Jessup, Cherry knew, had told Jon's mother to give him canned orange juice, cod-liver oil, and egg yolk from the time the baby was three weeks old. Cereal, puréed fruit, and vegetables should have been added to his diet long ago. But Mrs. Pansy White could not seem to follow the doctor's orders. She was one of those nervous, bewildered women who work hard all day but accomplish very little.

When Cherry and Eliza came into the one-room, untidy shack, little Jon was screaming at the top of his lungs. He was lying on the big bed, his scrawny body arched with pain. Colic again, Cherry decided, guessing that the baby probably had had something indigestible for breakfast instead of well-cooked cereal.

His mother, who had been hovering worriedly beside the bed, turned when she heard Cherry say, "Good morning, Mrs. White. I'd like to scrub my hands before I examine Jon. And would you let Eliza put some water on to boil? I think a warm, soapy enema will make him much more comfortable."

Pansy White forced a smile of welcome to her pale, thin lips. "Shore, an' I'll thank you both kindly. But nothen ain't a-goen to do this un no good 'cepten a dip in the spring." She ladled water from a big tub into a smaller one.

Cherry took soap and a clean towel from her satchel and thoroughly washed her hands. As she took the baby's temperature with her rectal thermometer, she said to Eliza, "Let the water boil three minutes and then take it from the fire to cool. I want it lukewarm and I'll need only a cupful."

Jon had a temperature of 103 degrees. Half an hour later, after an enema and an alcohol sponge bath, his temperature had dropped to 100. He was sleeping peacefully when Cherry left the room, followed by his mother and Eliza.

"I'll stop in again this afternoon," Cherry told Mrs. White. "In the meantime, don't give him anything but boiled, lukewarm water. If he wakes up and cries as though he were in pain again, send for me. I'm going from here to the Hendersons', then to the Bryans', and from there to the Hopkinses'. After that, I'll be at the Smiths'—around dinnertime. Unless you send for me before, I'll come back right after dinner."

Mrs. White nodded. "I thought maybe some catnip tea—" she began.

Cherry emphatically shook her head, smiling. "No catnip tea, Mrs. White, please. Just plain boiled water. Promise?"

The thin little woman nodded again. "But iffen he has worms—"

"He hasn't got worms," Cherry assured her. She and Eliza hurried along to see the Henderson baby. Cherry was delighted to find that teen-age Lily Henderson was carefully bathing her baby sister in front of the fire.

"Bertha larned me," she told Cherry proudly. "Maw an' the rest is out holpen Paw plant corn."

But when they stopped in next door they found that the Bryan baby had not yet been bathed. His mother had four other children under six and was only too glad to turn the baby over to Eliza.

Cherry left her there and went on to visit the last baby on her list. The little Hopkins girl was the prettiest one of the lot. She was not as robust as Baby Powell, but her cheeks were pink and her plump legs a golden tan from the sun baths her mother gave her. Mrs. Hopkins was working in the vegetable patch near the house, and the baby was lying on a folded quilt beside her.

"Did you have time to bathe Betty?" Cherry asked, smiling down at the pretty baby. "We don't want her to get that diaper rash again, you know."

The smile of welcome faded from Mrs. Hopkins' face. "Hit's mighty tedjus bathen her every day," she said evasively. "I give her that boughten food," she added, changing the subject. "She's a-gitten so now she likes it right well."

"Fine," Cherry said. "If you'd let me, I'd love to give her a bath."

"I don't hold with too much bathen," Mrs. Hopkins said firmly. "Hit's apt to weaken a body."

Cherry sighed inwardly. There was no point in discussing the matter further. She did not dare antagonize Mrs. Hopkins, for she had a six-year-old son who Cherry hoped would soon be enrolled in Bertha's "boarding school." Richard Hopkins was Billy Carter's boon companion. If any one of the children should be isolated, it was he.

The sun was high in the sky when she emerged from the woods and began the rocky climb to the Smiths' home. Through the window she could see old Mrs. Smith working at the big hand loom, her body swaying with the rhythm of the flying shuttle and the foot pedals.

The front door was wide open and the warm sunlight streamed into the huge living room. Young Mrs. Smith was setting the table for dinner. The two men were on the porch washing their hands. Cherry hesitated at the gate. Bertha had assured her that even the poorest family in Heartbreak Hollow welcomed guests at mealtimes. And it was considered an honor to entertain the doctor and his nurse. But Cherry had not yet grown used to the idea of dropping in without an invitation.

The gate creaked protestingly as she timidly opened it. Instantly, almost apprehensively, Lincoln Smith whirled in her direction. He was a powerfully built man with a thick crop of unruly black hair. He shaded his eyes from the sun with a big hand and glowered at her. Then he smiled and strode down the steps.

"Why, Miss Cherry," he greeted her warmly. "I 'low you walk as quietly as a cat on moss." Over one shoulder he called to his wife, "Bella, set another place fer Miss Cherry, an' dish up the vittles."

Dinner consisted of fried eggs, fried chicken, home-canned string beans, corn bread, biscuits, pickles, preserves, two kinds of pie, coffee, and large glasses of rich milk. The men ate silently and steadily, almost as though there was no pleasure in the business of stoking the furnace of their energies. After they had consumed large quantities of the rich, starchy food, they pushed back their chairs and left for the fields below the house.

Cherry insisted upon helping Mrs. Bella Smith wash the dishes. The old granny dried them and stacked them in the cupboards, chatting all the while. Ever since Cherry had entered the house she had been hoping for a chance to mention casually the poisoning of the Clarkes' hog. But Granny Smith, who ate practically nothing, had dominated the conversation at the luncheon table. Now at last she said something which gave Cherry the opportunity she had been waiting for.

Since there was no refrigeration in the valley, all perishable leftovers were scraped from the enormous platters into a deep slop pail. Cherry was appalled at the amount of delicious food that would be fed to the pigs and chickens. Why couldn't it have been sent to some poorer family? It was all she could do to keep from protesting when she saw a whole chicken and several untouched eggs disappear into that cavernous pail. And what about the creamy milk in the big earthenware jug? Wouldn't it be sour by night? The Wilsons had seven growing children but had neither a cow nor a chicken, and only a small plot of unfertile land. How those skinny boys and girls would have enjoyed the Smiths' "table leavens"!

Old Mrs. Smith must have noticed the horrified expression on Cherry's face, for she said, "I declare, Bella, them vittles you sarved Miss Cherry wan't hardly fit fer the hogs. The nex' time she draps in, you might put somethen on the cookstove more fitten fer a sprightly gal fotched in from the outside."

"Hogs?" Cherry repeated, wide-eyed. "Why, it was just about the most delicious meal I ever ate. And speaking of hogs, did you know that someone poisoned the pig the Clarkes have been fattening for months?"

The platter Mrs. Bella Smith had been holding above the garbage pail slipped from her hands and smashed to smithereens on the back-porch floor. The old granny sucked in her breath and let it out again in a loud, toothless whistle.

"It's jist as I was a-tellen you, Bella," she breathed. "The devil hisself has come back to this hyar hollow. And it sarves them Clarkes right. Them varmints," she hissed. "A-dirtyen up our wool!"

"Oh, I'm sure they didn't touch your wool," Cherry said quietly. "The person who played that cruel trick on you is the same one who poisoned their hog."

"An' who," Granny Smith demanded harshly, "might that pussen be, miss?"

"I don't know," Cherry admitted. "But it must be someone who doesn't want Bruce to marry Eliza. I was wondering if perhaps a jealous suitor is behind the mystery. Another young man who is in love with Eliza."

It was Mrs. Bella Smith who answered in a sad, low voice. "Eliza ain't never looked at nobody but my Bruce. They-all has been a-courten sence they was young'uns."

"An' unbeknownst to me," the granny said, with a sniff. "Iffen I had a-known, I'd a put a stop to sech goens-on. But that's neither hyar nor yander. The p'int is that their courten, against the vows o' their great-great-grandpappies, has brung Satan down upon us all. I seed the witches was vexed from the way they was a-flyen through the air las' night acrost the face o' the moon. An' afore that, I heerd Satan a-diggen an' a-diggen out in the ol' terbaccer field where nobody 'cepten sperrits has set foot sence the Clarkes an' the Smiths started a-warren. Diggen a grave, the devil was. Mine fustest, maybe, but he hain't a-goen to stop with me, I'll be bound!" Her wrinkled old face was an ash-gray as she mumbled one evil prediction after another. Mrs. Bella Smith stood staring at her, white to the lips, her long, gray eyes full of unhappiness. They had both apparently forgotten that Cherry was sitting behind them, her limp hands resting on the edge of the washtub.

Cherry felt limp all over. Was there anyone in the whole world who could cure this determinedly superstitious old lady of her convictions? Certainly, Cherry Ames, a "brought-on woman," had no chance at all.

"I warned you, an' I warned you," old Mrs. Smith was admonishing her granddaughter-in-law. "Iffen you had a-follered my advice an' braided cornhusks in the mules' manes, the ha'nts would-a stayed away instid a maken 'em prance an' snort all the livelong night, an' a-kicken down their stalls."

The granny stopped for breath and Mrs. Bella Smith said meekly, "Lincoln, he thinks somebody put somethen in their feedbins to make 'em carry on so. Somethen like they give horses in the bluegrass country to make 'em run real fast. Lincoln, he don't hold with your talk, Granny, that sperrits made 'em act up like they did."

The frail little old woman drew herself up to her full height, which made her no taller than the average ten-year-old child. "I never did hear o' sech trashy talk," she announced loftily. "How could sech outlandish horse medicine git in hyar from the bluegrass country?"

How could it, indeed? Cherry asked herself. And then she thought she knew the answer to all the mysteries. There was no one in Heartbreak Hollow who had any reason for making the old feud flare up—except Mr. Chase Spofford! Now that the Clarkes and Smiths were at war again, they would not plant tobacco in their long-idle field. Under the circumstances he might be able to buy the land at five dollars an acre.

Cherry bit her lip. That didn't make sense. Mr. Spofford was representing a philanthropist who surely had not commissioned him to hoodwink the people out of their land. Philanthropists just didn't work that way. Shrewd real-estate operators often rode roughshod over the rights of widows and orphans in order to buy land cheaply. But a kindly old gentleman such as Mr. Spofford was supposedly representing—

"*Supposedly* representing," Cherry repeated to herself. So far, the "city feller" had named no names. But when Dr. Jessup arrived next Saturday, Mr. Spofford would surely discuss with him all details of the proposed sanitarium. He would name names then, Cherry felt sure, and if Dr. Jessup suspected that anything underhanded was going on, he would check up on him by sending a wire or a letter to New York.

She sighed inwardly. Dr. Jessup would be so busy next Saturday that she doubted if he would show any interest in the flare-up of the old feud. The seven expectant mothers were due for checkups, and so were the five babies. They would all be weighed and given thorough physical examinations. Furthermore, in view of the fact that there could be no doubt now that Billy Carter had whooping cough, Dr. Jessup would want to spend most of his time and energy in the launching of the immunization program. Cherry hoped that Bertha's isolation ward would be established by then and that Dr. Jessup would approve of it. She also hoped that the magic word "school," even without a real teacher, might put the children's parents in a more receptive frame of mind. For the sake of "larnin' " they had allowed the older children to be given the "needle" several times. So perhaps, once they were convinced that Bertha was going to teach the six- and-seven-year-olds their three R's, they would permit them to receive the whooping cough vaccine. And Dr. Jessup would, of course, give each child diphtheria and antitetanus toxoid in the same injection, thus killing three birds with one stone.

Cherry rose from her stooping position by the washtub. Granny Smith's long list of maledictions had at last come to an end. She had prophesied the imminent death of all Smiths and Clarkes and that disaster would befall anyone even remotely related to them. Since most of the mountaineers were "kin" to each other, this included everyone in the hollow. She put away the last clean dish and suddenly noticed Cherry for the first time since the tirade began.

Instantly the pouting wrinkles changed into smiles. "Gracious, chile," she said, "you must be plumb wore out a-listenen to me a-faulten Bella."

A dull flush seeped through the whiteness of Bruce's mother's face. Cherry could not tell whether it was caused by suppressed anger or shame.

"I still don't think it's civil, Granny," she muttered, "fer Bruce to stop speaken to Eliza without cause. That poor gal's heart mus' be nigh broke. Iffen you could only feel to 'low him to 'splain the sarcumstances—"

"Git," her grandmother-in-law interrupted. She turned back to Cherry as Mrs. Bella Smith slowly walked down the path to where the men were plowing. "Kin you stop with me a minute?" the granny asked Cherry. "A body gets lonely sence I hain't hardly equal to doen much visiten these days."

"I'd love to visit with you for a while," Cherry said,

seating herself beside the old woman on the big, home-made sofa-bed. She told her first that Billy Carter had whooping cough. "His mother," she said, "would certainly appreciate it if you could help her out as much as you can. I know it's a long walk, down one hill and up another, but I thought perhaps if you were going down later to meet the mule train—"

"I'll go 'long down when you go," Granny Smith broke in. "An' take the night with 'em too if it 'pears to be needessary." She patted a pile of bright-colored blankets. "But I'd shore like to be in the big loom house when the mule train comes fer my kivvers."

"That's another thing, Mrs. Smith," Cherry began. "I know it's none of my business, and I hope you'll forgive me for asking, but I can't help wondering how much that store in Titusville pays you for the lovely things you weave."

"Five dollars fer the kivvers," Granny Smith said proudly. "Deborah Clarke don't get no more fer her hooked rugs an' it takes her twicet as long to do one."

"Five dollars?" Cherry repeated in amazement. She had seen machine-made wool blankets not nearly as lovely as these selling in big department stores for twenty dollars. The wholesale price was probably about two-thirds of the retail price. "Five dollars," she said again. "Why, Mrs. Smith, you ought not to sell them for less than fifteen dollars apiece."

The old lady's hooded eyes shot open with surprise. "I never did hear sech talk," she said, but added shrewdly, "Do you know where I kin sell 'em fer that?"

Cherry told her then about the Mai Lee project. Granny Smith listened attentively, every now and then nodding with approval. "That city feller," she interrupted once, "he paid me twicet as much fer them neckerchers as I'd-a got in Titusville. Two dollars he give me fer the two of 'em."

"In New York," Cherry told her, "there's a little store on the street they call Madison Avenue. They sell nothing but hand-woven wool neckties. The prices range from five dollars to twenty-five dollars. The ties you sold Mr. Spofford would be sold there for about fifteen dollars apiece. And the people who own the store probably would buy them from you for ten dollars." She didn't add that in another store across the street Granny Clarke's hooked rugs probably would be displayed in the window with price tags starting at thirty-five dollars.

"Sakes alive!" The little old woman hugged herself, rocking back and forth with delight. "I got a dozen kivvers thar, an' thar they stays till you hear from your friend on the outside." Her lips moved soundlessly as she mentally calculated her profit. Finally she said, "I hain't much good at figgeren, Cherry. What might the whole kit an' kaboodle bring us'n?"

Cherry counted the neat piles of ties, scarfs, and blankets. After a while she said, "I think if Mai Lee finds the right store, your family ought to be able to sell all these lovely things for more than five hundred dollars."

"Sakes alive," Granny Smith cried again. She reached

up to a wooden peg on the wall behind her and took down her black sunbonnet and shawl. "You an' me," she said in the authoritative voice of a general to his second-in-command, "we got to git down to the big loom house an' do some figgeren. Them poor demented folks cain't be 'lowed to send their kivvers an' kerchers off on the mule train no more."

Cherry could hardly believe that this victory had been won so easily. She didn't let herself think about what might happen if Mai Lee wrote back that she couldn't interest any store in Heartbreak Hollow's handicrafts. Mai Lee would just *have* to find the right place, or places.

Granny Smith tucked her clawlike hand through Cherry's arm as they started down the rocky path. She gave Cherry an affectionate squeeze. "My," she said, "I hain't had so much interest in liven sence I was knee-high to a grasshopper. I wan't much older'n Billy Carter when my Lije's paw tuck atter Lazarus Clarke with his shooten rifle. Afore a body could sing a ballat straight through, they was more folks kilt than was borned that year. I clumb a tree an' seen the fit, till my mammy come atter me with a hicker limb." She chuckled reminiscently. "I was already a-aimen to marry Lije then, an' he nothen but a chunk of a shirt-tailed boy. But mighty pleasen looken, though he never had no decent duds. Bruce, he takes atter his great-grandpappy. Iffen he wan't so contrarious, Cherry, he'd be my favrit offspring, he would. Why cain't he take a shine to that sprightly Pettit gal? The one with the purty red hair. What might her name be, Cherry?"

"Kate," Cherry said, thinking of little Jenny's big sister who was Eliza's chum. "Kate Pettit," she said softly, "wouldn't let Bruce court her even if he wanted to. She knows how much Eliza loves him. I think Eliza must love him as much as you did your husband."

Granny Smith coldly took her hand away from the crook of Cherry's arm. Then she replaced it. "You reckon she loves my Bruce that much?" she asked.

Cherry held her breath and nodded her head up and down. After a moment's silence, she said, "Another thing I think is that if your family had been feuding with the Smiths, you would have married Lije, anyway. You're a very high-spirited woman, Mrs. Smith, and I'm sure you were even more so when you were Eliza's age."

Again Cherry's arm was hugged affectionately. "And," she went on, "I think you're the smartest woman in this valley. I think you know it was a man, not the devil, who ruined your wool and poisoned the Clarkes' hog."

The little old lady sighed, obviously torn between flattery and superstition. When they stopped at the foot-log across the little creek below the spring, she said, rather belligerently, "If hit wan't the devil pizened that hog, who done it, Cherry? The Clarkes, for all that they is varmints, is well liked by the other folks. An' none o' my male offsprings left the house las' night. I know, 'cause I didn't sleep so good, what with that diggen a-goen on."

"Did you hear someone digging all night long?" Cherry asked in surprise.

"I shore did," the granny replied as Cherry helped her across to the other side. "An' I seed that it was Satan hisself, in his red duds."

"That's funny," Cherry reflected out loud without realizing it. "Granny Clarke thought she saw a devil sneaking by their barn early yesterday morning. I thought she imagined it. Her hands are badly twisted with arthritis. And pain, as you know, can cause people to see things that aren't there."

"Hit shore can," Granny Smith agreed. "Ary a soul told me that Deb Clarke was a-sufferen. I cain't bear nohow to hear 'bout a body haven pain, even iffen hit's one o' them, them critters." She stopped, embarrassed by her own sympathy, then blurted, "Truth o' the matter is that Deb ain't no Clarke. She was borned a Pettit, an' up ontel our weddens, her an' me was jist like this." She crossed two fingers and held them defiantly under Cherry's nose. "Guess I got a right to send her some o' my yallerroot tea, if I have a mind to. She niver could make hit proper herself."

"I think it would be a very nice thing to do," Cherry said in a humble tone of voice. As they walked along the narrow path through the woods, she added, "When you married Elijah, did he make you promise never to speak to your best friend again?"

The old lady sniffed. "Nobody made me promise nothen. Lije's mammy, she axed me iffen I'd take the vow, which I did, she bein' on her deathbed. But I didn't promise not to speak to Debby, 'cause she was still a Pettit then. She danced at my wedden, Deb did. 'Twas atter her own wedden that she stopped speaken to me." She tossed her proud old head. "Natcherly, atter she oncet passed me by 'thout so much as a nod, I done the same to her."

"Well, I think it's a shame," Cherry cried impulsively. "It all began when you were both little girls, and neither one of you had anything to do with the quarrel between the Clarkes and the Smiths. Oh, I do wish you two old friends would make up. You could have *such* fun visiting each other. And it would make a lot of difference if you would work together helping Dr. Jessup when people are sick and need you both."

Granny Smith stopped and pushed back her big black sunbonnet so she could peer into Cherry's face. "Land, chile," she exclaimed, "ary a soul ever put hit to me thataway afore! I hain't got no hard feelens fer Debby. An' iffen I was shore her grands an' greats was out o' the house I might drap in with that yallerroot tea myself."

"Oh, please do," Cherry begged. If the two old women spoke even one word to each other, their "grands" might well follow suit. Then the mystery of who was behind the flare-up of the feud might be solved in a short while.

For Cherry was sure that the man who disguised himself as a devil was neither a Clarke nor a Smith. It was all she could do to keep from confiding in Granny Smith that she suspected Mr. Chase Spofford. But Cherry knew that the wisest course was to move slowly with these people, taking but one small step at a time.

"Please go see Mrs. Deborah Clarke," she said again as they emerged from the woods. "Dr. Jessup would be ever so grateful if you could make her understand how much he needs you both in his work."

"I'll study on hit," the old woman promised. "I'll study on hit."

CHAPTER V

The Mule Train

THE MULE TRAIN, TO CHERRY'S ASTONISHMENT, TURNED out to be a half-track, a huge six-wheel truck equipped with tractor cleats on its four rear wheels. Bertha made no effort to disguise her delight at the stunned expression on Cherry's face when the driver, with a loud blast of his horn, appeared on the mountain road.

"I knew you expected a covered wagon," Bertha giggled. "Just as I did. I swear, if a helicopter flew in and out of here daily with mail and supplies it would still be the mule train to these die-hards."

"Granny Smith isn't really such a die-hard," Cherry said, almost shouting above the uproar as men, women, and children gathered around the truck in front of the community loom house. "Wait until she climbs up on that nail keg and delivers the speech she's been rehearsing all day!"

"Cherry Ames," Bertha cried accusingly. "Have you

been keeping secrets from me? Did you actually win her over to our side on the Mai Lee project?"

"Tit for tat," Cherry came back, laughing. "You kept the secret of the mule train from me, so—" Someone was tugging at her arm, and Cherry turned to look into Eliza's worried face.

"Oh, Miss Cherry," she cried. "Lu is bad sick, a-squirmen an' a-writhen somethen awful. Could you kindly come back with me now?"

Cherry nodded, and with Eliza close behind her, pushed her way through the crowd to the clinic across the road. There she snatched up her bag and hurried out to the porch. Bertha had hobbled as far as the steps and in her calm, reassuring voice was saying to Eliza:

"Don't worry, honey. It's probably nothing but a good old-fashioned stomach-ache. What did Lu have for supper?"

"Nothen," Eliza replied. "She ain't eaten a thing sence breakfast. Didn't seem to have no appetite. Maw said it was from plowen out in the hot sun. At noontime, when Lu wouldn't tech her lunch, Maw made her go an' lie down on the bed in Granny's room. I set right beside her atter that, an' she wouldn't even take a sip o' water. Then when she smelled supper cooken, she begun to gag an' retch, but nothen come up. She didn't have no pain till atter Maw an' Paw left to meet the mule train. 'Pears as though, soon as she heerd that horn a-blasten, the cramps begun." She smiled wanly at Bertha and set off at a fast trot beside Cherry, who turned around long enough to form with her lips one word and a big question mark:

"Appendicitis?"

Bertha shrugged. "Could be. But don't let it throw you," she said. "If necessary we can convert the mule train into a you-know-what." She formed the word "ambulance" with her lips.

Cherry sighed audibly with relief. It would be a rough ride over the mountains, but if an emergency operation was indicated, Lu would be in the Titusville hospital before midnight.

It was now eight o'clock and the almost-full moon shone brightly in the sky. As they hurried up the steep, winding lane, Eliza said tearfully, "If the angels take Lu, Miss Cherry, hit's my fault. Granny says the devil put a spell on her 'cause I was a-goen to marry with Bruce Smith."

"The angels aren't going to take your little sister," Cherry said, her voice rather sharp with impatience. "And no matter what is wrong with her, you and Bruce had nothing to do with it. You know that, Eliza," she added more gently. "Your granny is a wonderful old woman, and I respect her as much as you do. But you must realize that she never had the advantages that you have had. She never went to school, so when anything happens which she can't explain she naturally blames it on the devil. You know better, Eliza. You know what makes Dr. Jessup's helicopter fly. You know that the ghosts she sees in the early morning are nothing but dew rising in the form of fog. You know that witches have nothing to do with thunder and lightning. And you know, as well as I do, that neither a Smith nor the devil poisoned your hog or gave your little sister a stomach-ache."

Eliza said nothing. The mountain streams looked like silver Christmas ribbon in the moonlight. The air was cool and fragrant. Misty clouds, which even Cherry had to admit did look like anemic ghosts, floated across the face of the frosty moon. She tried to forget that down below important things were happening. Soon Granny Smith would be delivering her speech, guaranteed to convince the men and women who had worked hard all winter in the community loom house that they must delay shipment for another month. After that, Bertha would probably call a meeting of the Parents-Nurses Association and present the idea of a kindergarten and first-grade boarding school.

Those events were important for the good of the entire community, but, at the moment, nothing was as important as the fact that a little girl, only a few years younger than harum-scarum Midge Fortune, was in pain.

Cherry could hear Lu's moans even before she climbed the steps to the porch. Without bothering to knock, she pushed open the heavy front door and hurried inside. Eliza darted ahead of her to lead the way into Granny Clarke's spacious room. There, on the huge four-poster bed, Lucretza Clarke lay, writhing. Her red-gold curls, a heritage from the Pettit side of her family, were damp with sweat. Her strong, but skinny little hands were white-knuckled with pain. She looked up, glassy-eyed, as Cherry moved quietly across the room and sat in the chair Eliza drew up to the bed for her.

When the spasm passed, Lu smiled bravely. " 'Tain't nothen, Miss Cherry," she said. "Somethen I et, no doubt." She frowned at her great-grandmother, who was crouched on the other side of the bed. "Granny, she's bin a-tryen to tell me that the devil has got into my insides, but I don't hold with sech trashy talk. An' I ain't aimen to tech none o' her nasty-tasten tea. Won't do me no good nohow."

The twelve-year-olds, Cherry reflected, were indeed the coming generation. They, and they alone, consistently dared to defy the superstitious edicts of the old grannies. And for Lu to do so now, amounted to sheer heroism. Cherry lightly touched her fingers to the child's thin wrist. "Where does it hurt you most, honey?"

With her free hand, Lu pointed to various spots on her abdomen. "Sometimes hyar, sometimes thar."

Cherry shook down her thermometer and handed it to Lu. "You've had your temperature taken before, darling," she said. "Under your tongue and way back, remember?"

Lu nodded, and lay quietly for two minutes, watching the second hand on Cherry's wrist watch. Then she proudly handed the thermometer back to Cherry. The mercury had stopped at 99.

"You have hardly any fever at all," Cherry said, smiling. "Look, you can see for yourself. The silver line stopped just a teeny bit beyond the red arrow."

Granny Clarke spoke then for the first time. Professional jealousy had kept her from greeting Cherry, and fear, Cherry suspected, had kept her from interfering. High-spirited Lu was her granny's favorite offspring. The little redheaded hoyden, she often said, was a "true Pettit."

"In-*strew*-ment o' the devil hisself," Granny Clarke muttered suddenly, pointing a shaking hand at the thermometer. "Magic, black magic."

Lu, who had begun to relax from the moment Cherry came into the room, giggled. "Silver, Granny," she said pertly. "Hit's what outside folks call mercury."

As she talked, Cherry examined her lithe little body from head to foot. It was almost impossible to diagnose appendicitis in the early stages without a blood count, but after a thorough examination, Cherry felt reasonably sure that Lu's discomfort was caused by the useless bit of anatomy in the lower right part of her abdomen. It was there that Cherry's probing fingers had discovered the symptomatic tenderness. But there was no sure way for Cherry to determine whether or not an immediate operation was indicated. The next spasm passed so quickly that Lu merely clenched her hands for a second and then resumed her saucy conversation with her great-grandmother. After that, she suffered no more pain for almost an hour.

As she watched and waited, Cherry couldn't help wondering where Lu's parents were. Surely, even such a momentous event as the arrival of the mule train couldn't keep them away from their sick child. Finally she asked Eliza:

"Didn't you tell your father and mother that Lu was having pains in her tummy when you came to get me?"

Eliza shook her head. "Paw an' Maw don't have much fun 'cepten when they's a meeten in the loom house. They don't know much about doctoren nohow. An' I figgered they might stand betwixt you an' Lu iffen you had a mind to give her the needle."

Cherry stared at her with respect. Meek little Eliza, it seemed, had more independence than she had at first thought. In a sense, she had deliberately excluded her parents from the sickroom so that they could not stand in the path of modern medicine. Where there was such intelligence and independence, there was hope. Eliza might yet throw off the shackles of the superstitious Clarke matriarch, and marry Bruce. That is, if Bruce, in his turn, would dare to defy his own granny.

Then Cherry was struck with another thought. How had Eliza planned to keep Granny Clarke from interfering if Cherry had, for instance, had the authority to give Lu an injection of morphine to relieve her pain?

As though reading her mind, Eliza went on to explain. "Granny," she said rather proudly, "she hain't so much agin your doctoren now sence she seen how hit didn't make little Billy Carter no worse."

The little old woman sniffed. "He's still a-whoopen an' a-coughen," she informed Cherry arrogantly. "Least ways, he was up till an hour ago when Eliza come to fotch me home."

"But he didn't turn black in the face like you 'spected," Lu broke in. "An' the angels ain't a-goen to come fer him nor fer me neither." At that she kicked off the quilt and dangled her straight, thin legs over the edge of the mattress. "I ain't got them green-apple gripes no more. I'm a-goen down to the loom house, I am, an' see the mule train."

Cherry laughed as she firmly tucked the comforter around the child's bare legs. "It's all right for you to sit up if you keep covered. But you've got to stay quietly in bed until we're sure the mercury in my thermometer isn't going to go up any higher."

Lu frowned petulantly and promptly appealed to her great-grandmother. "That's all foolishness, ain't it, Granny? I don't have to stay in the bed iffen I don't feel to, do I?"

For answer the old woman glared at her. "You hain't goen to do no traipsen fer a considerable spell," she muttered darkly. "You was bad sick, Lu, an' iffen Eliza hadn't done what she done a while back, they's no tellen how long the devil might-a kep' his pitchfork in your stommick."

Cherry sent Eliza for a glass of water. Then she opened her satchel and took out a white envelope. Lu sat up and watched with interest. Gently Cherry unclenched the child's hand and shook into the palm of it two aspirin tablets.

"I want you to swallow these with just a sip of water," she told Lu, hoping that the child was not too nauseated to obey.

"I kin chew 'em up an' swaller 'em down without no water," Lu said airily.

"No, don't do that," Cherry said, smiling. "They have a bitter taste, almost as bitter as your granny's feverweed tea. But if you swallow them with a little water they won't have any taste at all."

"What kind o' pilts is them things?" Granny Clarke demanded, leaning across the bed suspiciously.

"The same ones," Cherry told her quietly, "that Dr. Jessup gave you. In a little while Lu should go to sleep. If we don't disturb her, she may even sleep the whole night through and wake up tomorrow feeling fine and well again."

"I hope so," Cherry added to herself. "Otherwise, she goes to Titusville on the mule train."

As she sat beside the bed, waiting for the aspirin to take effect, Cherry mentally counted on her fingers. The four nights and three days between now and Dr. Jessup's next visit seemed like a long time. Perhaps she should send the child to him in the morning, anyway. But suppose Lu's discomfort had been caused by nothing more than a mild disturbance in the intestinal tract?

Then Dr. Jessup, a very busy man, would be saddled with a perfectly well child until he could fly her back home on Saturday.

On the other hand, after the mule train left at dawn, there would be no way of communicating with the doctor. Suppose the pains persisted, indicating inflammation? Waiting too long for surgery might mean a ruptured appendix. If only the clinic were equipped with a laboratory where Cherry could determine whether or not there had been any increase in the white cells in Lu's blood!

The child was sleeping peacefully before Cherry finally came to the conclusion that she and Bertha could not make a decision until the very last minute. She tiptoed out of the room, signaling to the granny and Eliza that they must follow.

The logs in the huge stone fireplace were smoldering embers now, and the big living room was chilly. Eliza quickly and deftly built up the fire again. Granny Clarke planted herself on a stool just outside the door to her bedroom.

"I ain't aimen to sleep none," she told Cherry. "You go 'long with you an' git some rest. 'Tain't no needessity fer both o' us to set up all night."

Cherry smiled at her gratefully. "I'll go down to the loom house now and have a talk with Bertha, and Lu's parents. Then I *will* go to bed, but you must promise to send for me if Lu wakes up and has any pain. And, most important of all," she told them both, "she mustn't have *any*thing to eat or drink. A sip or two of plain water won't do any harm if she cries for it, but nothing more than that."

Granny Clarke tossed her head. "I hain't a-goen to dost the child, iffen that's what you're a-feerd of. 'Pears like them little pilts o' yours worked mighty fine," she added grudgingly.

"Granny," Eliza asked meekly, "could I kindly go 'long down with Miss Cherry? I won't be gone no longer than a minute or two."

"Shore, chile," old Mrs. Clarke said fondly. "An' you stay fer the dancen. Your mammy kin come home now an' take keer o' her own chile, I reckon. An' like as not, that Wrangel boy with the bright yaller hair is a-pinen fer to dance with you."

Eliza said nothing until after she and Cherry were halfway down the lane. Then she suddenly burst into tears. "I cain't keep my promise, Miss Cherry," she sobbed. "I cain't."

"What did you promise, Eliza?" Cherry asked quietly. "Did your granny make you promise again that you wouldn't even smile at Bruce?"

"More than that," Eliza wailed. "When Lu was took with real bad pains, Granny said the devil would keep his pitchfork in her until I put Bruce clear out o' my mind. I promised I wouldn't never give him another thought, but I shouldn't-a said them words, Miss Cherry, 'cause I cain't put him out o' my mind nor out o' my heart."

"Of course, you can't," Cherry said, torn between pity and anger.

A shadow moved out of the bypath that led to the spring. "Evenen, Miss Cherry," Bruce Smith said in a low, taut voice. "I was a-wonderen if you might kindly tell Eliza that I heerd what she said, an' I cain't put her out o' my heart nor my mind neither." He turned and strode back into the shadows.

Cherry drew Eliza's arm through hers. "Let's go down to the mule train and buy your shoes," she said. "I have a feeling that things will work out so you and Bruce will get married after all."

Eliza had stopped crying the minute she heard Bruce's voice, and now she moved along beside Cherry as though walking in her sleep. Suddenly she squared her shoulders and said defiantly, "I ain't a-goen to put Bruce out o' my heart nor out o' my mind. I ain't a-feerd o' the devil."

"Of course you're not," Cherry said. "You made that promise because you were worried about your little sister. But you might as well forget it, for you couldn't possibly keep it. Naturally, you'll obey your parents and not speak to Bruce until they give their consent, but they are too intelligent to ask you to put him out of your thoughts. You must remember that your granny is a very old lady, Eliza. Old people sometimes say and do things that are, well, childish."

"I know," Eliza said, with a swift smile. "But I don't

hardly dairst buy no shoes, Miss Cherry. Besides, I got ary a grain o' money."

Although Cherry wanted, with all her heart, to lend the young girl enough money for her wedding shoes, she didn't dare risk hurting her pride. Such an offer might well be interpreted as an insult. She glanced down at the small brown feet.

"She probably wears a 5 A," Cherry decided. "The same size I do. I'll buy myself a pair of shoes just in case. If things work out the way I hope they will, Eliza will accept them as a wedding present."

Cherry fully realized that she was pinning her hopes on the slim chance that Granny Smith might soon call on her girlhood chum. Even if that happened, she couldn't, of course, be at all sure that a reconciliation between the two might take place. But Deborah Pettit Clarke just might accept Martha Smith's "yallerroot" tea with a "Thank you very kindly." In that case the spell would be broken. In her mind's eye, Cherry could see the two old cronies gossiping for hours on end. Once they got together they would throw an occasional "Scat!" in the direction of their grands and greats, who might then assume that the old feud had at last come to an end. Then it shouldn't take long for Josh Clarke and his son, Malcolm, Lincoln Smith and his son, Bruce, to discover the identity of the cruel person who had been playing tricks on both families.

At that moment, the person whom Cherry suspected

came out of the loom house and stood on the porch. His hands were clenched tightly at his sides, and in the bright moonlight she could see that his face was contorted with rage.

Cherry and Eliza stopped by the clinic steps, for Bertha was sitting there, her injured leg stretched out in front of her.

"How's Lu?" she asked.

"Sleeping peacefully," Cherry said. "More of that anon. How did you make out?"

"We won," she told Cherry gleefully. "Granny Smith and I both won. Not even a necktie goes to Titusville on the mule train tomorrow. And the boarding school opens as of dawn!" She chuckled. "Mr. Spofford tried to argue against the Mai Lee project, but nobody listened. I wonder why he's so much against the idea."

"I can guess," Cherry said as Eliza hurried on to join her parents. "Nobody's going to sell a foot of land as long as there's a chance they'll make much more money selling something else."

Bertha glanced at her sharply and then turned to stare at the man who was standing, taut with anger, on the loom-house porch. "I see what you mean," she said thoughtfully. "I see what you mean!"

CHAPTER VI

Bertha's Boarding School

CHERRY FELL ASLEEP TO THE SOUND OF A FIDDLE AND banjo rising above songs and laughter. The merrymaking in the community loom house continued far into the night. But she and Bertha slept soundly through the noise and awoke long before dawn.

Cherry's first thought was of little Lu Clarke. "Well, what's the verdict?" she asked Bertha as they hurriedly dressed in front of the blazing logs. "Does Lu go or stay?"

"She obviously had a good night," Bertha said, frowning with concentration. "And if when you get there you find that her temperature hasn't gone up, I'd say she stays. We both know that a great many people survive any number of chronic attacks of appendicitis before they finally get around to having the pesky things taken out. Dr. Jessup will bring his portable lab with him when he comes Saturday. After a blood count he can decide whether the case is operative or not. And, after all, as I keep saying, Lu may not have had anything more than a good old-fashioned stomach-ache. Pork doesn't sit well on a lot of people, and kids Lu's age are apt to bolt their food."

"That's true," Cherry said. "If it weren't for the tenderness on her right side, I wouldn't worry at all." She went out to the well for a pail of water and hung it from the chimney hook above the logs. "I'm not going to wait for coffee," she told Bertha. "I'm afraid that half-track might drive off before I've taken Lu's temperature."

"Wait a minute," Bertha said calmly. "Let's check our wrist watches. Then, if all is well up at the Clarkes', go out on the porch and press the button on your flashlight three times. On the dot of six. I'll be watching from the porch down here. Then you can stay on for breakfast and go on to the Carter child and Pansy White's baby without coming back here at all."

"Fine," Cherry agreed. Then she suddenly remembered something she had forgotten during the excitement of the night before. She took a crisp five-dollar bill from her wallet and handed it to Bertha with a grin. "Before the mule train leaves, will you buy me a nice, pretty pair of shoes, size 5 A?"

"No soap," Bertha replied, grinning back at her. "I thought of that myself. But there wasn't one pair of shoes in that truck. The driver knows the people here only buy them in the fall." She patted Cherry's hand.

"Don't count your chickens before they're hatched, honey. I don't honestly think there'll be a wedding in Heartbreak Hollow this month."

Cherry shrugged. "Well, order a pair for Eliza so they'll be sure to come on the next delivery, won't you? And don't forget our important mail!"

It was still dark when Cherry arrived at the Clarkes' home, but the area around the fireplace in the living room was alight with the flames from the huge logs. The whole family had gathered there, including Lucretza, who was frying pork chops in an enormous skillet.

Cherry mentally counted to ten. This situation was going to be difficult. How was she going to convince Lu's parents that the child should stay in bed and have nothing to eat or drink except sips of water for the next twenty-four hours? Nobody in Heartbreak Hollow had ever heard of appendicitis, and their knowledge of anatomy was so limited that she knew any attempt at an explanation would be useless.

It was the old granny who greeted Cherry first. "Mornen," she said cordially. "You're mighty welcome. Our least'un, as you kin see, is as spry as a grasshopper agin. An' as hongry as a hoss. I 'low iffen she gits some good hot vittles into her, she kin git back to her plowen."

Eliza's mother beckoned Cherry to a splint-bottomed chair near the fire. "Set," she said, her voice neither cold nor warm. "We-all is jist about to et, an' it would be a pure delight to have you jine us."

Her husband, Josh, smiled at Cherry, but stared at her rather suspiciously, she thought, combing his short curly beard with one big roughened hand.

Eliza came in then from the back porch carrying a pail of water. She glanced at Cherry, who had seated herself stiffly on the chair, and said with a surprising show of spirit:

"I tried to tell them, Cherry, I tried, I did. But Lu, she commenced to holler—"

"I didn't holler," Lu broke in, speaking for the first time since Cherry had appeared at the door. "I didn't do nothen 'cepten tell Maw I was hongry."

"It doesn't matter," Cherry said in a soothing voice. "I know you're hungry, honey. I am too. But let's first take your temperature, shall we? Will you go in and lie on your granny's bed while we do it? Here, you can take my flashlight and show me the way."

The flashlight did it. Lu set the skillet down on the hearth so quickly that grease splashed out, spluttering noisily. A thermometer was an interesting instrument, but not to be compared with that rarity, an electric torch. Lu lay quietly under the comforter, the thermometer in her mouth, but her whole attention was concentrated on flashing the light on and off. Cherry glanced at her wrist watch and, in spite of her worries, remembered with a rush of homesickness that her twin Charlie had given it to her when she went into training. She had known then that she was embarking on a career that might take her anywhere and into some apparently impossible situations, but she had never even dreamed that she might one day have to battle the superstitions and customs of the eighteenth century.

To her relief, Lu's temperature was normal. And it was one minute before six. Should she allow the child to go out on the porch and flash the good news to Bertha herself? It would seem like part of a game to Lu, and it might make her feel that she was in a conspiracy with the two nurses, sharing a secret with them.

Cherry wiped the thermometer with cotton soaked in alcohol. "The silver line," she told Lu, "stopped at the red arrow. I told Bertha, who is waiting down at the clinic, worrying about you, that I would let her know if the silver line stopped at the arrow, by going out on the porch and pressing the button on my flashlight three times. Would you like to wrap up warmly in this lovely strawberry quilt and do it for me? You shouldn't really get out of bed until tomorrow morning, you know. But I think Bertha might stop worrying about you if she knew that you flashed the light yourself."

Lu kicked off the comforter and hopped to the floor. "I'll do hit fer you, Cherry. An' I'll wrop myself in the kivver like you said, tho' it ain't hardly cold a-tall." She giggled and scurried out on the porch looking like an enlarged version of the needle pumice in Cherry's mother's sewing basket.

Thinking about her mother made Cherry homesick all over again. How would *she* have handled a situation like this where very little nursing ability and a great deal of tact were required? Then Cherry remembered something. Once when she and Charlie had been rebellious little convalescents of twelve, their mother had kept them in bed by putting them to work.

"Listen, children," Mrs. Ames had said seriously, "I know you both feel well enough to ride your bikes and go back to school, but Dr. Fortune says you must stay in bed a few more days."

Dr. Joe Fortune had brought Cherry and Charlie into the world. They loved and respected him, so they had listened quietly as their mother went on, "Dr. Joe is a very busy man. Here in Hilton he has several sick children to take care of, children half your age, who, like you, feel well enough to get up but who should stay in bed a little longer. I thought you might like to help Dr. Joe by making some games which would keep his little patients busy until they can go back to kindergarten."

Cherry remembered what fun she and Charlie had had making puzzles. They had pasted maps and pictures from magazines on cardboard and had cut them out in big odd-shaped chunks. Cherry had labored over a map of the United States, each piece of the puzzle a separate state. Then, at the last minute, tiny Rhode Island had disappeared. Cherry had been on the verge of tears until Charlie, howling with impish laughter, had produced it from the pocket of his pajama jacket. The time, Cherry remembered, had passed so quickly that even after the twins were allowed out of bed, they had remained quietly in their rooms for several hours finishing some of the puzzles they had started earlier in the week.

Why wouldn't the same scheme work with Lu?

Young Mrs. Clarke, although stubborn and sullen at times, was really very kindhearted and community-minded. In her taciturn way she had told Cherry the evening before how much she approved of Bertha's plan for a boarding school and had offered to let Eliza help out as often as she could be spared. Perhaps now, if appealed to tactfully, she might be willing to lend Lu to Bertha for three or four days and nights. If so, Bertha could then keep Lu in bed and on a bland diet until Dr. Jessup arrived. And Lu, in return, could help Bertha keep the younger children amused.

After the signal to Bertha had been successfully sent, Cherry led Lu back to her granny's bed. Then she told her her plan. Lu crowed with delight.

"I kin larn 'em how to read an' write an' spell," she told Cherry proudly. "I'm real good, I am."

Her mother, who had apparently been listening outside the door, came into the room then. "Lu," she said to Cherry with unusual enthusiasm, "is a pure scholar. She's aimen to be a teacher-woman like Miss Scope, an' she will do hit, too. Her paw says iffen we don't get a teacher here soon, he's a-goen to send Lu to Titusville. She's plumb ready for high school, tho' she don't allus talk like hit."

"I kin talk jist like Miss Scope and Cherry and Bertha when I have a mind to," Lu interrupted. "And so kin Eliza." She sat up in bed and said in a parrotlike voice, "I can teach the little'uns how to read and write and spell, because I'm a scholar, and I plan to be a teacher when I grow up."

Cherry laughed. "You'll make a wonderful teacher, Lu. Do you want to start today? I'm sure your father will carry you down to the schoolhouse if you ask him very nicely."

"I kin walk," Lu said with a toss of her head.

"I really don't think you ought to," Cherry said, her mouth smiling but her eyes frowning. "Suppose your insides got jiggled up and started to hurt again? Then Bertha would have to take care of you instead of you helping her take care of the little ones."

"Josh, he'll wagon her down," Mrs. Clarke said succinctly. "Malcolm kin come over an' finish up the plowen. Iffen Lu is a-goen to larn his leetle Henry, his wife kin shorely spare him to give us a hand fer a day."

"Malcolm's here now," Eliza said from the doorway. "Henrietta heard Lu was bad sick an' sent him over to holp."

Josh Clarke came into the room, followed by his tall, gentle-faced married son. Malcolm Clarke, Cherry was sure, had never hurt even a fly in his life. He bobbed his head at her and said in his gentle voice, "I jist brung Henry an' his bed down to the schoolhouse, ma'am. The desks is all moved out an' most o' the beds an' chilluns is in."

"How wonderful," Cherry cried. The sky above Old Desolate was still only faintly rosy with dawn, and yet Bertha's boarding school was already an accomplished fact. These people appeared to move slowly and deliberately, but once they decided to do something, it was done with record speed.

"The Wrangels' chickens," Malcolm went on with his report, "is a-pecken in the front yard alongside one o' the Pettit cows. An' David Wrangel is a-plowen up the land in back."

Lu held up her thin arms to her big brother then. "You wagon me right down thar, Malcolm. I'm a-goen to larn—to teach the young'uns."

Cherry quickly scribbled a note of explanation to Bertha and gave it to Lu. "This is like a report card," she said. "It explains what you *can* do and what you *can't* do to help Bertha."

Eliza drew Cherry aside then. "I'm a-goen," she began and then, speaking more slowly, started all over again. "I'm going down with Lu to help Bertha. Ma said I could. The plow-ing and the plant-ing is most done."

Cherry squeezed her hand affectionately and hurried on up the lane to the Carters' house. Not until then did she remember what Granny Clarke had said the night before. They had been talking about Billy and she had said:

"He's still a-whoopen an' a-coughen. Leastways, he was up till an hour ago when Eliza come to fotch me home."

So old Mrs. Clarke had disobeyed orders! Cherry, in her concern for Lu, had not grasped that fact at the time, and now she was struck with another thought. When Cherry had last seen her late yesterday afternoon, Granny Smith had been climbing up this very lane to call on Billy and his mother.

The two old cronies must have met in Billy's room! What had happened? Granny Clarke had obviously stayed on until evening. Had her presence driven Granny Smith away?

Cherry could not believe that any human being was capable of driving old Mrs. Smith from any place. And she had assured Cherry that except for the hour or so she planned to spend at the loom house delivering her speech, she would not leave Billy Carter's side.

"I'll take the night with them, too, if hit 'pears to be needessary," she had said. She had also said in answer to Cherry's plea that she make up with her old friend, "I'll study on hit."

Had she been thinking it over as she slowly climbed up this lane after rehearsing her speech? Had she come to the conclusion that she had a perfect right to speak to "Debby Clarke if she had a mind to"? Then, on the heels of her decision, she had probably found herself face to face with her girlhood chum.

What had happened?

Consumed with curiosity, Cherry almost ran the rest of the way. She had to stop for breath by the time she reached the Carters' yard. Before she climbed the steps,

Mrs. Carter came out on the porch, her face wreathed in smiles.

"Law, Miss Cherry," she said, " 'tain't no need fer you to hasten so. Billy's doen middlen well. Coughed most o' the night, but never woke up oncet an' had ary a whoop. He's bin a-whoopen some this mornen, but nothen to amount to much."

She came down the steps then and Cherry could see that she was fairly bursting with gossip. "Law, Miss Cherry," she said again. "You should of bin hyar yes-tiddy atternoon. Them two old grannies!" She threw her apron over her face and sank down beside Cherry, shaking with laughter.

"So you couldn't keep Granny Clarke away?" Cherry asked. There was no point in worrying about the fact that the old lady had deliberately exposed herself to a disease that might prove fatal. The chances were good, as Dr. Jessup himself had said, that Mrs. Clarke probably had, without realizing it, had a light case years ago.

"Keep her away?" Mrs. Carter demanded, chuckling as she wiped her streaming eyes with a corner of her apron. "Why, you had scacely drapped out o' sight afore she come stompen up the hill an' into the houseroom. I couldn't noways think of axen her to leave then, Miss Cherry. Wouldn't-a bin civil. And then, like you promised, soon atter dinner, Granny Smith comes along. She stomps right into the houseroom where Granny Clarke is a-setten on Billy's bed, an' I'd like to die o' fright when I seen her. It was so quiet-like fer a spell you could-a heerd a pin drap. Then all of a sudden Granny Smith ups an' says:

" 'Howdy, Debby. Heerd tell you was ailen. I bin aimen to bring you some o' my yallerroot tea.'

"Granny Clarke didn't say nothen right off. But atter a bit, she says, 'Hit's gone on nigh sixty year, Marthy, sence you spoke to me. What might be your reason fer doen hit now?'

"Granny Smith takes off her sunbonnet an' fans herself with hit, smilen. 'The way you talk, Debby! 'Twas you who stopped a-speaken to me fust.'

" ' 'Tain't so,' Granny Clarke hollers.

" ' 'Tiz!' Granny Smith hollers back." Mrs. Carter rocked back and forth, choking with laughter. "I hain't never heerd nor seed nothen like it, Miss Cherry. It was a pure sight! The way them two went on examinat-in' each other."

"I wish I could have seen them," Cherry said, with a grin. "I suppose the whole misunderstanding started years ago when one of them passed the other without seeing her. When I'm busy or in a hurry I often pass people I know very well without seeing them. But since neither I nor they belong to feuding families, it doesn't matter."

Mrs. Carter nodded understandingly. " 'Pears like neither o' them never promised not to speak, one to t'other. But they is a-speaken now!"

Cherry hardly dared to ask the question on the tip of

her tongue. "Do you think the feud is over, then, Mrs. Carter?"

Billy's mother shook her head. "No, Miss Cherry. Them two is agreed that the devil has come back in this hyar valley 'cause Bruce was a-courten Eliza." She shivered slightly. "They both seed him."

"Oh, dear." Cherry sighed. "Granny Smith still can't think Granny Clarke has that money. Aren't they agreed now that it must have been destroyed in the fire that started in the woods at the time of the feud?"

Mrs. Carter shrugged. "The onliest thing Granny Smith said about that was, 'Deb, hit hain't fitten fer our greats to git married till, accorden to their great-grandpappies' vows, that money is divided up equal 'twixt the Clarkes an' the Smiths. Has you got hit?' Then Granny Clarke says she hain't never seed ary a grain o' hit. Then Granny Smith talks about somethen else." She shivered again. "Mostly about the devil."

Cherry thought for a minute. Granny Smith was a shrewd old woman; even shrewder, in Cherry's opinion, than Granny Clarke. Since the ancient misunderstanding between the two had now been cleared up, Granny Smith must have come to the conclusion that the money was either lost or had been destroyed. For, if her husband had ever had it in his possession, Granny Clarke would have known about it. She might have kept it a secret all these years out of spite. Kentucky mountaineers often harbored grudges throughout a lifetime, and

Granny Smith's husband had insulted Granny Clarke's by insinuating that he was a liar and a thief. If the two brides had been on speaking terms three generations ago, they might well have been able to patch up the quarrel between their husbands. Then both families might have searched for the money—and found it.

According to the legend, no one had ever looked for it except Lazarus Clarke's offspring, and they had evidently confined their searching to their own property. Cherry closed her eyes and let her imagination carry her back to that day three generations ago when the feud had started. She could almost see Lazarus Clarke riding down the mountain trail on his mule, singing and shouting because his saddlebags were weighted down with "pay money." At his insistence, the tobacco auctioneer had probably paid him in coin, for even now the old mountaineers viewed paper money with suspicion. The mere sight of ten thousand dollars in gold and silver must have been cause for celebration throughout the whole hollow. There must have been dancing and merrymaking until dawn. And then, when the time came for the money to be divided up into equal shares, one angry word had led to another.

Long before the first shot was fired, Lazarus had undoubtedly hidden the money in some safe place. Where? "Where would you have hidden it?" Cherry asked herself. Later, after she had made her rounds, she asked Bertha the same question.

The vegetable garden behind the schoolhouse was a hive of activity. Men and boys were raking the plowed and harrowed land. Little girls were carrying away the rocks that were piled up in the four corners of the field, trundling wheelbarrows as easily and as expertly as other little girls push doll carriages.

Bertha, perched on a nail keg with her injured ankle resting on a big lard can, was sorting through the tattered, dog-eared primers. "Where would I have hidden that ten thousand dollars?" she repeated, smiling. "I would have poured it into this nail keg, and then I would have buried the keg in a hole in the ground."

"A keg or a barrel," Cherry said, nodding. "But where would you have dug the hole?"

"Some place where it was easy to dig," Bertha said promptly. She pointed to the red-brown earth of the garden. "A plowed field."

"That's what I think," Cherry said. "The tobacco crop had just been harvested. The money belonged to both families. Wouldn't some spot on those twenty acres be a logical place to dig? My point is that Lazarus Clarke and Dolph Smith, heads of the families, probably buried the money together before the celebrations began. And *I* think that they would have buried it on land that belonged to both of them—*not* in the woods on the Clarke property."

Bertha stared at her thoughtfully. "I see what you mean," she said slowly. "When the smoke cleared, both

Lazarus and Dolph were dead. And from that moment on, no one has ever disturbed the soil of the land they worked together."

"I could be wrong," Cherry said soberly, "but I'll bet the money is buried there. And if the feud hadn't flared up this week, the men might have plowed the field and found it."

Bertha sighed. "It gives me goose pimples to think about it. I can almost believe that the devil has something to do with it all. The red-tailed monster wants to keep the money for himself."

Cherry laughed. Then she leaned forward to whisper, "A devil *has* got something to do with it. An unfeeling monster, a fiend, if you ask me. Someone who is so greedy that he thinks nothing of ruining other people's lives in order to get what he wants."

Bertha's mouth fell open with surprise. "Cherry," she gasped, "you're so mad you frighten me."

Cherry's dark-brown eyes flashed. "I *am* mad," she told Bertha. "Look at Eliza's sad little face. Look at the misery stamped on Bruce's. Think of how terrified Granny Smith was the other night—why, she might have had a stroke! And remember how much that poisoned hog and ruined wool meant to both families."

Bertha clamped her mouth shut grimly. After a moment, she said, "You're right. The devil incarnate caused that feud to flare up. The devil in the form of our slick-haired 'city feller'!"

CHAPTER VII

Motives

"MR. CHASE SPOFFORD," CHERRY SAID EMPHATICALLY, "is the only one around here who has any motive. I strongly suspect that he plans to swindle the philanthropist he is representing, if there is such a person. As long as the Smith-Clarke land lies idle, he has a good chance of buying it at five dollars an acre. But he won't tell his employer, if any, that. He'll report that he had to pay much, much more for it, and pocket the difference himself."

"Wa-it a minute," Bertha begged. They had left the schoolhouse grounds and gone to the clinic porch in order to discuss their suspicions without fear of being overheard. "Why do you keep dropping tantalizing little phrases like 'if there is such a person,' and 'if any'?"

"Because," Cherry said, "last night when he was playing Santa Claus with the candy he bought from the mule train, I had a little chat with him. Tactfully, I hope, I led the conversation around to the spring, and I asked him what was the name of the man who planned to build a sanitarium here. He smiled in that condescending way of his and said, 'My dear, the gentleman in question does not wish his name divulged.' "

"So what?" Bertha demanded. "People like the Rockefellers and the Guggenheims donate millions which the public never hears about."

"Not millions," Cherry corrected her, smiling. "How do you suppose the Guggenheim Memorial and the Rockefeller Foundation got their names? It's not that great philanthropic families like that want publicity, but they know that their names are of almost as much value as their money. The building of a public sanitarium is not at all the same as sending Christmas turkeys to the poor. And I can't help thinking it's downright suspicious that the 'gentleman in question doesn't want his name divulged.' "

"Well, I don't," Bertha said flatly. "The whole project isn't even yet an architect's blueprint. The gentleman might well not want to divulge his name until he has the deeds to the land around the spring. Besides," she went on, "if no philanthropist is backing Mr. Spofford, what is he doing here? What possible use can he have for the water in the magic spring?"

"None whatsoever," Cherry admitted. "Except as a screen to disguise his real purpose, which is to buy as cheaply as possible the fertile Clarke-Smith land. I suspect that the 'gentleman in question' may be one of those rich, but not so philanthropic, cigarette companies which grow their own tobacco."

Bertha pursed her lips. "I see what you mean. The Clarkes and the Smiths are not stupid. If they had an inkling that someone wanted to buy their land in order to grow tobacco on it, they'd never sell . . . not at five dollars an acre."

"They certainly wouldn't," Cherry said. "And if you ask me, Granny Smith already smells a rat. That little old lady is the most fascinating blend of the old and the new! She took to our Mai Lee project like a duck to water. And I'll bet it was she who got Granny Clarke's vote."

"How I would love to have been there to watch those two old cronies hobnobbing together," Bertha cried. "I still can't believe it. Cherry Ames, you accomplished more in four days than I did in as many months."

"I haven't accomplished anything," Cherry said. "And I don't see how I can do a thing to prevent Mr. Spofford from swindling these people, as well as his employers, if that's his game. My only hope is that when Dr. Jessup meets him, he'll decide to investigate."

"He might," Bertha said, "but I doubt it. You've solved so many mysteries in your brief career, Cherry, that you're able to smell a rat a mile away. But Frank isn't like that. He takes people at face value." She hobbled down the steps. "Well, I'd better get back to my boarding school. Kate and Eliza should be starting lunch now in the loom-house kitchen."

"I'll just leave my bag inside and go over to help them," Cherry said. "How on earth are we going to keep Lu on nothing but water all day?"

"That's your problem," Bertha said, with a grin. "She's your patient."

Cherry darted inside the clinic and then hurried to catch up with Bertha. "Lookee, lookee," she said, displaying a four-ounce bottle with a medicine dropper cap. "Lu can have this much water every hour. I'm going to give her a pad and pencil and tell her to write down the number of drops she takes every quarter hour, and then when she's added up the total she'll know how many drops there are in four ounces."

"Fine," Bertha said. "That'll keep her happy for an hour. But then what?"

"That," Cherry said, with a mischievous smile, "is up to you, little schoolmarm. You could, of course, keep the game going all day by asking her to figure out the number of drops in a pint, quart, gallon, jug, lard pail, water bucket—"

"Stop," Bertha pleaded. "That would require algebra, and all I remember about that is 'Let x be the unknown quantity.'" She chuckled. "Unknown is right!"

"Seriously though," Cherry said, "I don't think we'll have much trouble with Lu. I'll sit with her while the other kids go over to the loom house for meals. I think she might enjoy patching up those primers with some of that Scotch tape I see you're hoarding in the clinic."

"Hoarding nothing," Bertha said indignantly. "I bought those rolls yesterday for the very purpose!" She giggled. "And what about those colored pencils you're hoarding? Seems to me that if I'm going to correct papers you ought to swap them with me in exchange for the Scotch tape."

"It's a deal," Cherry said, laughing. "To use your own words, I bought them for the very purpose. Also, some gold and silver paper for stars which Lu can make and cut out. Furthermore, I had the presence of mind to order some flashlight batteries, which I'll bet you didn't."

"I completely forgot in all the excitement," Bertha admitted ruefully. "The ones in my torch are getting pretty weak, too."

"You're as bad as I am," Cherry said. "Last night I had every intention of buying Eliza's shoes. I hope you didn't forget to order them this morning."

"I didn't," Bertha assured her. "But I'm not as optimistic as you, Cherry. "Those grannies will never let Bruce marry Eliza until the money is found."

"I know it," Cherry said calmly. "That's why we've got to find it."

"We?" Bertha demanded. "You and who else? I'd do almost anything for you, Ames, except dig for buried treasure with a sprained ankle."

"You don't have to dig," Cherry said airily. "Your job will be to put a bee in Granny Clarke's bonnet. My guess is that she'll spend a lot of time in the schoolhouse, now that her favorite offspring is one of your boarders. She likes you, but she barely tolerates me. If anyone can persuade her to agree to a truce, it's you."

"Truce?" Bertha repeated. "I don't get it."

"A temporary cessation of hostilities," Cherry said, with a grin. "The cessation to last long enough for the four men of the two families to spade up the Clarke-Smith land near their homes. I don't think Lazarus and Dolph carried ten thousand dollars in coin very far out into the field before they buried it, do you?"

"No," Bertha said, "but I think *you're* carrying things too far, Cherry Ames. We don't even know that Lazarus was paid in coin or that he buried it in the old tobacco field. If you don't watch out, you'll be building a hospital with that money before it's found!"

Cherry laughed. "I know I'm taking a lot for granted, Bertha," she admitted meekly. "But I may be able to find out one thing for sure. Granny Smith, even though she was only a little girl at the time, might remember whether Lazarus was paid with paper money or gold and silver. She told me herself that she climbed a tree to watch the battle."

"I can believe that," Bertha said, chuckling. "She must have been a hoyden in her day. She's a terror right now. And I still don't understand how you got so chummy with her."

"My famous cheeks," Cherry said. "Red is her favorite color. If Eliza had Lu's hair, I think Granny Smith might even allow Bruce to marry her."

Bertha shook with laughter. "I suppose you ordered some dye along with the flashlight batteries. Or a wig. When you shave Eliza's head I'll know it's time for me to have you locked up."

But Cherry wasn't listening. She was thinking about a devil's costume. One of the many suits of red flannel underwear, which always seemed to be hanging out on the clotheslines to dry, would make a very convincing devil's costume—especially in the moonlight. It would be so easy to borrow one and have its loss attributed to a sudden gust of April wind. Where would the "devil" who dug at night hide his costume in the daytime?

Under the mattress on the bed in the Clarkes' spare room, she decided. If only she could get in there and search it!

She and Bertha were standing now in front of the open door to the schoolhouse. Lu, from her cot by the window overlooking the garden, called to them.

"Bertha," she yelled. "Cherry! I'm hongry."

"Take it away," Bertha told Cherry, grinning. "I'll go around in back and fill the washing bucket so the kids can scrub their hands before lunch."

Cherry hurried inside to Lu. The schoolhouse had been swept and scrubbed from floor to ceiling. Someone had stuffed clean rags in the chinks in the log walls. The glass windowpanes, which had been bought the night before, shone like diamonds in the sunlight. All along the walls were neat little cots, each one boasting a gay, clean quilt. They formed a colorful chain, linking themselves to Bertha's larger bed in the middle. On it was Granny Clarke's beautiful strawberry quilt.

"My, how lovely everything looks," Cherry said to Lu. "Did you bring your granny's quilt down as a present for Bertha?"

Lu shook her head up and down. "Brought the bed, too, along with mine. Leastways, Malcolm did when he wagoned me down. It was the extry one in our spare room, you know."

"But what about Mr. Spofford?" Cherry asked. "Isn't he staying at your house any more? He wasn't there at breakfast, but I thought that was because he was still asleep."

"He was still asleep," Lu said, "an' he is still stayin' with us. They was two beds in that room." Swiftly she corrected herself. "*There were* two beds in that room. I've got to start talken like you an' Bertha an' Miss Scope if I'm goen to teach the little ones."

"Good for you," Cherry said absent-mindedly. She couldn't help thinking, "If only the Clarkes had made a mistake and had moved Mr. Spofford's bed. Then when they rolled up the mattress—" But that was silly, wishful thinking. Furthermore, he may not have hidden his devil's costume under the mattress. It might not even be he who was masquerading. She couldn't be absolutely sure until she had some concrete evidence.

"I want to start teachen right away," Lu was saying restlessly. "Cain't I, Cherry?"

Cherry swiftly came back to earth. "Not today,

honey," she said. "We've got to get things ready first. This afternoon the children are going to help plant the garden. While they're doing that, Bertha wants you to mend the books. And I want you to do some arithmetic for me."

She gave Lu the medicine bottle and explained again that she must have nothing but water all day, and only a few drops at a time. "There are four ounces in this little bottle," she said. "Do you know how many ounces there are in a pint?"

"Sixteen," Lu said promptly. "An' they—there are two pints in a quart an' four quarts in a gallon."

"Why, you're wonderful, Lu," Cherry cried, genuinely surprised. "Can you multiply?"

"Course," Lu replied. "I know all my tables."

"Well, then," Cherry said, "when you find out how many drops there are in this bottle you'll be able to figure out how many there are in a gallon."

She took a little pad and pencil from her pocket. "These are for you so you can tell me tonight before you go to sleep how much water you drank. I don't want you to have more than a quart, and it would be better if you had less." From another pocket she took a tube of bouillon cubes, a package of lemon junket, and a package of strawberry gelatin. "Tomorrow," she said, "if you're as well as you are today, you can have broth and custard and gelatin. I bought these from the mule wagon last night just for you."

Lu stared open-mouthed at the "boughten food."

The big red letters on the gelatin package fascinated her. Then she was captivated by the tinfoil wrapping on the bouillon cubes. After that she carefully read the directions on the junket package.

"What's lukewarm mean?" she demanded. "I got a cousin named Luke."

Cherry explained. "In order to be sure the temperature of the milk is just right, we drop a little of it on our wrist, just as we test the milk in a baby's bottle. If the milk is too cold or too hot when we stir in the powder, we won't have custard. We'll just have lemon-flavored milk."

The other children had finished lunch by the time Lu had read and digested the instructions on all the packages.

"I can do fer myself tomorrow," she said. "Fixen this boughten food is easy as fallen off of a log."

"It certainly is," Cherry agreed. "And after Dr. Jessup sees you on Saturday, he may say that you *can* do for yourself. But until he does, Lu, I can't let you get out of bed." Tears welled up in the child's eyes. Cherry went on quickly, "We mustn't waste time talking. We've got to mend the books. Over in the clinic is some nice sticky paper which you can see right through when we paste it over the torn pages. Shall I go get it?"

Immediately Lu brightened. "Scotch tape," she said. "Miss Scope had some. Billy Carter made off with it an' got his eyelashes stuck to his eyebrows."

They giggled together, and Cherry said, "I'm glad

you know how to use it. I'd like to stay with you all afternoon and help you mend the primers, but I can't. I have to see Billy and his little nephew, Jon White. It's funny to think of Billy being an uncle, isn't it?"

Lu arched her sandy eyebrows. "Funny? What's funny about that? I was aunt to Malcolm's little Henry when I was Billy's age. I was six when he was borned."

"That's true," Cherry said, still laughing. "I think I'll call you Aunt Lu after this."

Lu clapped her hands with glee. "An' I'll call you Granny Cherry."

And then, her clasped hands clutched to her stomach, she doubled forward with pain.

CHAPTER VIII

Mr. Spofford Eavesdrops

CHERRY'S HEART SANK. LU'S RED-GOLD HAIR FLOWED over her drawn-up knees as the pain knifed through her. And then the spasm passed as quickly as it had come. Lu raised her head and stretched out her legs, smiling.

"Don't think anythen of that, Cherry," she said. "I have them pains every now an' then. Sometimes I have 'em for a spell, an' sometimes only one. Las' night was the onliest time they was real bad."

Cherry tried to smile back. More and more it looked as though the diagnosis was going to be chronic appendicitis. Any hour now it might become acute. Oh, why hadn't she sent the child to Dr. Jessup on the mule train?

"How long have you been having these pains?" she asked.

Lu frowned with concentration. "I had some at the Halloween party, but Maw said it was from too much punkin pie. Thanksgiven I threw up most o' what I et, but I had et considerable, so Maw didn't pay it no mind. 'Twixt then an' Christmas, I had a spell o' pains, but I didn't say nothen—anything about hit to no—anybody."

Cherry sighed. "You should have told Dr. Jessup, honey." She waited for a while, and then when the pains did not recur, went over to her room for Scotch tape, colored pencils, scissors, and the gold and silver paper. Bertha brought in the tattered primers, and Cherry left them working together.

She was worried about little Jonathan White, who was sniffling in earnest. Whooping cough nearly always started out that way. Furthermore, tonight the moon would be full, and his mother was bound and determined to dip him in the icy waters of the spring.

When Cherry came into the house she found the child placidly sucking on a piece of fried fat back. For a moment she almost lost her temper. Only a few hours ago she had reiterated the fact that Jon should have nothing today but skimmed milk and weak gruel. She had arrived in time to fix his breakfast and feed him, but suspected that as soon as she had left, Mrs. White had supplemented his diet with a bit of corn pone.

"What did he have for lunch?" she asked, gently taking the greasy piece of white pork fat from the baby's mouth. "Did you fix his precooked cereal the way I showed you, Mrs. White?"

Above the scream of rage from Jon, his mother said

tiredly, " 'Pears like I cain't do proper with that boughten food, Miss Cherry. I biled it an' biled it, but it got so lumpy-like 'twan't fitten fer humans, so I give it to the pigs."

Cherry swallowed her impatience. "You weren't supposed to cook it at all, Mrs. White. Remember? I simply added warm, skimmed milk to the cereal and stirred it until it was smooth. Would you like me to show you again how to fix it? It's really very easy."

Mrs. White shrugged and said sullenly, " 'Tain't no needcessity. His paw done give him a drap o' everythen on his plate at noon. Said there was nothen wrong with the young'un, 'cepten he was hongry fer a man-person's vittles."

Cherry bit her lip. Daniel White should have known better. He was one of the most intelligent young men in the hollow, but he was as stubborn as a mule. He respected Dr. Jessup and barely tolerated the two nurses. Women, in his opinion, were not supposed to think. He knew that his wife was a very inadequate mother, and often interfered when she tried to dose little Jon with vile-tasting concoctions. Furthermore, he had stated flatly that his son was not, under any circumstances, to be dipped in the spring. The grannies and their superstitions had no terrors for him, but he had his own ideas on how children should be reared. He himself, from the time he started to cut his first tooth, had always had a taste of everything on his father's plate. It was a tradition in his family that the baby must have something solid to chew on in order to hasten the teething period. In vain had Cherry pointed out that Jon had started to teethe at a much earlier age than the average infant. A six-month-old baby might have been able to digest what Jon obviously could not.

He was now screaming not so much from temper as from pain. Only a warm, soapy enema would put him out of his misery. But Cherry could tell from the stubborn light in Pansy White's eyes that, in spite of her husband's edict, she was going to dip her baby in the spring that very night.

Suddenly Cherry had an idea. Perhaps if she used water from the magic spring for the baby's enema and sponge bath Mrs. White might be satisfied.

"Jon," she said patiently, "has colic again, and I want you, Mrs. White, to give him his enema and alcohol rub yourself. You saw how comfortable they made him yesterday. And do you think it might be a good idea if we used the water from the magic spring? You can't, of course, dip him tonight because he has a cold."

Some of the stubbornness went out of Pansy's eyes. Without a word, she took a pail from a wooden peg above the fireplace and left the house. Cherry picked up little Jon and held him to her shoulder, patting and gently rubbing his back. When Pansy came back she hung the pail on a hook above the flaming logs. With dogged but sullen determination she followed Cherry's directions until at last the puny boy was sleeping peacefully.

Then suddenly, without any warning, she threw her arms around Cherry and hugged her. "I knowed I was wrong, Cherry," she said shamefacedly, "not to do what you tole me to. An' I'm a-goen to take good keer o' Jon atter this. You don't have to come back no more an' do fer him. I kin do fer him myself."

"I know you can," Cherry said softly. "And you're too smart to think that bathing him in the spring water at midnight will do him anything but harm. If I were you, I'd bathe his little insides with it, instead. Let him drink as much of it as you can get into him, but be sure to boil it first, won't you?"

Mrs. White nodded and added wistfully, "I'd shore be purely delighted iffen you'd larn me how to take his temperature. Dan'l, he knows how to read that thar in-strew-ment real good, but I cain't seem to get the knack nohow."

"I'll show you how this evening when I come back around suppertime," Cherry promised. She hurried along the bypath to the lane that wound up the hill to the Carters' big home. Mrs. White's new attitude was very encouraging, but Cherry wasn't at all sure how long it would last. If only she could somehow impress Daniel White with the fact that his small son should be kept on a bland diet for a few days! Dr. Jessup, she realized, was the only one who could accomplish that feat. Somehow on Saturday she must arrange the day's program so that he could have a talk with Daniel.

Billy Carter's temperature was still normal and he seemed well and happy in spite of the fact that he still whooped occasionally and had vomited twice that day.

"I didn't lose nothen to amount to much," he told Cherry proudly. "When kin I git out o' bed?"

"After Dr. Jessup sees you on Saturday," Cherry told him. "He's the boss, you know." She told him then about the school and how Lu Clarke was mending the books. "Lu has to stay in bed, too," she said. "Would you like me to bring you some of her colored pencils so you can draw pictures? You can see the cow and the chickens from your window."

He wriggled excitedly. "I'd shore like to draw a pitcher o' the sun a-goen down behind the hills," he said. "All red an' gold an' purple, the sky is then. *So* purty."

Cherry made up her mind to buy drawing paper, crayons, and paintboxes when the mule train came again. A lot of the children were probably starving to express themselves through the medium of color. They were starving for so many things other children took for granted!

After charting Billy's TPR, she left him. Now for a visit with Granny Smith!

The little old lady greeted Cherry warmly and, with much cackling laughter, described her reunion with Granny Clarke. As soon as she tactfully could, Cherry led the conversation around to old Lazarus Clarke.

"Do you remember, Mrs. Smith," she asked, "whether he was paid for the tobacco in paper money or coin?"

"Gold," the granny said promptly. "I seed it myself. He poured hit into a barrel, I ricollect, whilst we all stood a-watchen. It was a pure sight."

"And then," Cherry went on quietly, "don't you think he and your father-in-law buried it somewhere together? Not in the woods on the Clarkes' property, but in the field that belonged to both families. A hollow tree would be the logical place to hide a wad of paper money, but if you wanted to hide a barrel full of coin, wouldn't you bury it, Mrs. Smith?"

"I shorely would," the old granny said, slapping her knee emphatically. "I don't know why we never suspicioned that before. An' Lije's paw, I'll be bound, holped with the buryen, too. Lije, he was jist a shirt-tailed lad then, an' didn't do no figgeren. He jist took hit into his head that Lazarus' son knew whar the money was hid but wouldn't tell."

"If he had known," Cherry said, "I think he would have told his wife, don't you?"

Granny Smith nodded. "Deb never did see ary a grain o' hit. In my jedgment, hit's what you suspicion hit is. In the old terbaccer field!"

Cherry held her breath. Did she dare suggest a truce now, or should she move more slowly and let the little old lady come to that conclusion herself?

"The devil put a curse on that money," Granny Smith

was muttering. "He wants hit for hisself. An' when he heerd Linc say t'other day him an' Josh was a-goen to plow the field, he got scairt, Satan did, fer fear one o' the grands or greats would find hit fust. That's why he spends most o' the night a-diggen, I'll be bound."

"Did you hear someone digging again last night?" Cherry asked curiously. The person who had been masquerading as the devil had already accomplished his purpose. The feud had flared up very satisfactorily. There was no reason for him to continue annoying this little old woman and at the same time risk having his identity discovered.

And then her heart sank as she realized that the "devil" might not be digging for the purpose of frightening old Mrs. Smith. He might be digging for gold! Chase Spofford was shrewd enough to have followed the same line of reasoning that had led Cherry to the conclusion that the money was buried on the land that belonged to both families.

"I heerd him an' I seed him," Granny Smith was saying. "An' the sooner he finds that money an' gits out o' here, the better hit will be fer all o' us Smiths an Clarkes."

"Oh, but we mustn't let him find it," Cherry pro tested impulsively. "Your grands and greats must find it first. It belongs to your families."

"Hit belongs to the devil," Granny Smith said stubbornly. "I wouldn't tech ary a grain of hit." Adroitly she changed the subject. "I bin aimen to go down to the schoolhouse all mornen," she said, reaching up for her shawl and bonnet. "I'll go 'long down with you now. Then I'll visit fer a spell with Billy Carter so his maw kin do her washen. 'Pears like the wind blowed his paw's red flannels off the line Monday while she was nursen him."

Cherry jumped. So a suit of red flannels *was* missing. "I don't think the wind blew them off the line," she told Granny Smith as they started down the hill arm in arm. "I think a man stole them. The same man who dresses up like the devil and spends most of the night digging in the old tobacco field. The very same evil man who ruined your wool and poisoned the Clarkes' hog."

Granny Smith trotted along beside Cherry just as though she hadn't heard a word. "Hit was mighty windy Monday, I ricollect," she said stubbornly and again changed the subject. "Heerd tell Debby's leetle Lu was took real bad sick las' night. I'm mighty sorry, even though the young'un is a Clarke. An' the devil hain't a-goen to stop with her. He'll git us all afore he's through. Bruce had no business goen against his great-grandpappy's vow."

"But, Mrs. Smith," Cherry argued without much hope, "your husband wouldn't have made that vow if he had found the money. Now that you think it may be buried in the old field, won't you encourage Bruce and his father to search for it?"

The little old lady stopped and placed her hands

firmly on her hips. She threw back her head to peer solemnly up at Cherry. "There wan't no feuden an' fighten in this hyar valley ontel the devil brung in that money. I aim to let him take hit out agin."

Cherry sighed. If only she had some proof that the "devil" was Mr. Chase Spofford! Cherry was sure that if Granny Smith shared her own suspicions she wouldn't let *him* take the money out of the hollow.

Suddenly Cherry made up her mind. At the risk of losing the little old lady's friendship, she had to drop a hint. "Mrs. Smith," she admitted humbly, "on the way over here from the Carters' I trespassed a little. Someone has been digging in that field. Someone who left behind the footprints of a man; not the cloven hoofprints of the devil."

The veined lids that hooded the old woman's faded blue eyes shot up. Thoughtfully she stroked the ribbon on her sunbonnet. She tucked her other hand in the crook of Cherry's arm. "You is a mighty knowen woman," she said, "fer all that you hain't more than a girl chile. I'll ponder on what you said erbout letten Linc an' Bruce do some diggen. But how is we a-goen to git Debby to let Josh an' Malcolm dig alongside o' them? We-all cain't set foot in that thar field onless the Clarkes is party to hit."

"I know," Cherry said, trying not to show how excited she was. *"One step at a time, Ames,"* she counseled herself. "I thought you," she said slowly, "might put a bee in Mrs. Clarke's bonnet. She barely tolerates me," she added, with a rueful smile. "I wouldn't dare say things to her that I feel free to say to you."

Mrs. Smith tossed her head, obviously flattered. "Deb allus was set in her ways. I'll speak to her, fust chancet I git, erbout you. She hain't got no cause fer faulten you. 'Pears like you didn't do Billy Carter no harm when you give him them pilts. To be f'ar an' squar' Debby ought to give the devil his due."

She chuckled as Cherry helped her across the footlog. Side by side, they walked into the fragrant woods. "The devil," she mumbled. "A man pussen's footprints. Zeke Carter's missen red flannels. I don't aim to let no city feller make off with that money."

And then, as they came around a bend in the path, they found themselves face to face with Mr. Chase Spofford. Cherry guessed from the guilty expression on his face that he had been standing there, eavesdropping, for some time. She could only hope that he had not been able to hear the words Granny Smith had just mumbled.

"Oh, hello, Mr. Spofford," she said, forcing her lips into a smile. "Have you been over at the schoolhouse helping Miss Larsen? She was counting on you to put up that barrel hoop for the little boys' basketball team."

"I would have been glad to oblige," he said affably. "But without a basketball I didn't see much point in it."

"But we have a basketball," Cherry told him. "I saw it in the supply box around lunchtime when Miss Larsen was unpacking the books. She got the truck driver to fill it with air before he left this morning."

He shrugged. "He must have put so much air in it that it took off like a balloon. Or, what is more likely, some child took it home."

"That's ridiculous," Cherry said tartly. "The children here don't take things that belong to the school."

"The children here," he said, with a supercilious smile, "are like children everywhere. They're all little magpies." He turned to Granny Smith. "One of them apparently couldn't resist those handsome ties I bought from you. I strongly suspect Billy Carter, because I was staying in his home when they were stolen. But since the child is ill, I won't accuse him."

Granny Smith glared at him with her hooded eyes. "Billy hain't got no use for neckerchers. Him an' his paw hain't got a shirt with a collar 'twixt 'em."

He laughed. "But such a pretty color. All children love red. At least, so I'm told." He bowed to Cherry. "They have all fallen in love with you because of your rosy cheeks, I imagine."

Cherry flushed. "Children," she said coolly, "have better sense than most adults. They like people for what they are, not because of how they look."

"Oh, come now," he said, smiling. "Lu Clarke worships the ground you walk on. But if you were not a very pretty young woman, I doubt if she would be such a tractable little patient. Like most redheads, that child has a fiendish temper."

Granny Smith interrupted then. " 'Pears like we all cain't stop talken about red—an'—fiends." She brushed past him. "Come on, Cherry. I don't aim to waste the day conversen with a city feller who has ary a grain o' sense."

With a brief smile to Mr. Spofford, Cherry followed her around the bend. They walked through the woods in silence. When they reached the clinic well, Granny Clarke said in a loud whisper:

"Him an' his ornery notions! Git me the wish book, Cherry. I aim to buy the chillun 'nother ball with the money he give me fer them neckerchers. You do the writen. The doctor-man kin carry the letter to Titusville Satiddy."

The "wish book," Cherry had learned the night before, was a mail-order catalogue. "You're very generous, Mrs. Smith," she said, "but I don't think we really need to order another ball. The one Miss Scope bought will show up sooner or later."

The little old lady sniffed. "Iffen you should ax me, I'd tell you right out that the pussen who tuck hit was that city feller."

"Do you really think so?" Cherry asked. "But why?"

"Jist to be ornery," Mrs. Smith replied emphatically. "He 'cused Billy o' stealen them neckerchers jist to be ornery. He says Lu Clarke is a mean young'un, jist to be ornery." She jammed her small fists into the pockets of her snowy-white apron. "The devil," she said ominously, "don't always go around in red duds. Sometimes he 'pears to us in the form o' a human. Iffen he comes acrost a pussen with a black heart, he makes a deal with him. They swaps bodies fer a spell. My granny knowed a man oncet who sold his body to Satan fer a poke full o' gold. The onliest way he could git his own body back was to harness Satan to his plow an' turn up a field with him stid o' his mule."

Cherry didn't know whether to laugh or cry. This lovable little old lady was such a complex mixture of the old and the new! She wouldn't, Cherry felt sure, allow a human being to take the Clarke-Smith money out of the valley. But a human masquerading as the devil was something else again.

A distant clap of thunder broke the stillness in the valley. The puffy cumulus clouds that had been scudding across the blue sky all day had piled up into gigantic, threatening thunderheads. Rain was falling in huge drops by the time Cherry and Granny Smith reached the schoolhouse porch.

"I hope it rains all night," Cherry said to herself, "for then there won't be a moon. And little Jon White's dipping will have to be postponed." She crossed her fingers. "Even Satan himself wouldn't dig during a downpour."

CHAPTER IX

A Ghostly Apparition

CHERRY'S WISH WAS GRANTED. THE RAIN DIDN'T LET UP until late Friday night. The hillside streams became raging torrents, and the mudholes where the pigs usually wallowed all day turned into lakes. She trudged along roads ankle-deep in mud and climbed up dangerously slippery paths. Even when the rain slanted down in what seemed like solid sheets of water, she visited Jon White and Billy Carter.

After the first huge drops fell, Granny Smith had decided to "take the night" with the Carters. Cherry was grateful because the monotonous patter of the rain on the roof above his head made Billy fretful. Granny Smith kept him amused with stories which he illustrated, using the colored pencils and paper Cherry brought to him.

Little Jonathan's sniffles had developed into a heavy cold. Although his temperature never rose above 100, the sound of his tortured breathing panicked his mother. Cherry could guess from the terrified expression on Mrs. White's face that she had made up her mind to dip the baby in the magic spring as soon as the moon came out.

"I'm tempted to kidnap Jon," Cherry told Bertha, "and keep him until the moon wanes. His mother's being very good about his diet, and, believe it or not, she has learned how to read a thermometer. But she is firmly convinced that his cold is an exaggerated symptom of 'the teething sickness,' for which there is no cure except a dip at midnight when the moon is full."

Bertha stared disconsolately out the window at the schoolhouse garden. "It's an ill wind," she said, "that blows nobody good. This rain has washed away all our seeds, but it has probably kept Jon from pneumonia." She cleared her throat. "I'm hoarse from reading to the kids, Cherry. And I'll bet they're bored to death with the sound of my voice. What else can we do to keep them amused?"

"Games," Cherry said. " 'London Bridge Is Falling Down,' 'Ring-around-a-rosy.' We could mark squares on the floor with chalk and let them play Hopscotch."

"Don't even mention the word 'hop,' " Bertha said, with a moan. "That's all I do from morning to night."

Lu, from her bed behind them, interrupted then. "I feel sick," she said. "Terrible sick. Oh, oh, I'm going to throw up."

And she did.

"That does it," Bertha whispered to Cherry later as

they made up the bed with clean sheets. "It's appendicitis for sure."

Cherry glanced at her wrist watch. It was five o'clock Friday afternoon. Dr. Jessup would not arrive until nine the following morning. And unless the downpour let up he would not arrive at all. No one, not even Frank Jessup, would risk flying over those fog-capped mountain peaks.

Just in time she placed a basin on the pillow beside Lu's white face. From then on the child vomited at intervals, but she had no pain. The tenderness in the lower right side of her abdomen had markedly increased. Between the attacks of nausea she wept bitterly.

"I wanna go home. I want my maw. I want my granny."

Then miraculously Eliza appeared at the front door, soaked to the skin, her molasses-colored hair dark and straight. Without even waiting to wring out her skirt, she dashed between the rows of beds to Lu's side.

"Eliza," Lu wailed, "take me home. NOW!"

Bertha and Cherry left them alone together for a moment. "This is apt to go on all night," Bertha said. "We can't keep her here. The other kids wouldn't sleep a wink. But we can't move her in the pouring rain."

"I know," Cherry said, "but it can't rain forever. It's just got to stop, Bertha. If Dr. Jessup doesn't fly in tomorrow, what will we do?"

"I'm not even going to think about that," Bertha said

flatly. "Right now we've got to help Eliza convince Lu that she can't go home. If and when the rain stops, her father can come down and carry her over to my old bed in the clinic. After that, you and I will have to take turns sitting with her until Frank comes. Which he will," she added, going out on the porch. "It's beginning to let up a little now, Cherry."

But not until eleven o'clock did the rain stop entirely. The sky was dark, except for a few pale stars, when Lu's father carried her over to the nurses' quarters behind the clinic. The child was too exhausted to cry by then, and she dozed between the violent attacks of nausea.

Cherry and Bertha had done the best they could to prepare her parents for Dr. Jessup's diagnosis. They both felt sure that he would want to fly Lu to the Titusville Hospital as soon as possible after his examination. Josh and his wife had listened with expressionless faces when Cherry tried to explain that an appendectomy was nothing to be feared.

"Lu won't have to stay in bed more than a day," Bertha had added. "She'll be home next week, better than new. Two weeks from now she'll be plowing and she won't have any more of those pains."

"Nobody hain't a-goen to put no knife in my least-'un," Mrs. Clarke said stubbornly as Cherry tucked Lu in Bertha's big bed. "Soon as she stops throwen up, I'll give her some sulphur an' molasses. Ain't nothen wrong with her 'cepten she et too many dumplens t'other day."

Bertha came in then and said patiently, "No laxatives,

Mrs. Clarke. I explained that to you, remember? Lu can't even have water until Dr. Jessup sees her." She touched the older woman's shoulder sympathetically. "Why don't you go home and get some rest, Mrs. Clarke? Cherry and I will take good care of Lu. We both love her, you know that." She turned to Josh Clarke. "If you approve, Eliza will stay in the schoolhouse with the other children so I can be with Lu."

He nodded. Lu woke up, gagging and retching. Mrs. Clarke began to sob. Firmly Josh led her out of the room. Cherry followed them as far as the porch. A high wind had swept away the mist, and the moon was now shining brightly in the star-studded sky.

Cherry thought she had never seen a more completely full moon in her life, and at the same time she thought of little Jon White. In less than an hour it would be midnight. Was Pansy White watching the moon now as her husband slept? Was she planning to take the baby in her arms and tiptoe out of the house as the "witching hour" drew near?

Lu had fallen asleep again when Cherry returned to the bedroom. "Bertha," she whispered, "the moon is full and in twenty minutes it will be midnight. Is there anything I can do to keep Jon's mother from dipping him in the spring?"

"Sure," Bertha whispered back. "Go over there. If things look suspicious, all you have to do is accidentally on purpose make enough noise to wake up Pansy's husband. Daniel will cope with the situation after that." She grinned. "I've been cooking up that scheme ever since the first star came out."

"You *are* a mighty knowen woman," Cherry said approvingly as she tucked a flashlight in her sweater pocket. A few minutes later she was climbing the slippery road that led up the hill to the Clarkes', and their next-door neighbors, the Carters.

Cherry was halfway up the hill and was just about to turn off into the bypath when she heard a scream. At first she thought it came from the Clarkes' big stone house, but when the shrill scream again broke the night's stillness, she knew that it was someone at the Carters'.

And then, as she stared up at the sprawling frame house, she saw something that almost brought a scream from her own throat. A frightening apparition hovered in mid-air between the barn and the lean-to, its legs and arms flapping in the breeze. It had a face with an evilly grinning mouth and slits of eyes that faintly glowed in the moonlight. It danced away from the lean-to and suddenly disappeared as it neared the roof of the barn.

By the time Cherry had scrambled the rest of the way up the hill, Billy's parents and Granny Smith were out in the yard. Josh Clarke was shouting up from his own porch, "Anyone in trouble? Need holp?"

"I hardly think so," Mr. Carter called back. "Granny Smith jist got scairt by one o' her own witches."

" 'Twan't no witch," the old woman said crossly. "Hit was the devil with his fiery eyes an' mouth. I seed 'em jist as plain."

"I saw it too," Cherry said to the Carters. "Someone tied the thing to the clothesline and used the pulley to make it dance back and forth between the shed and the barn. Whoever played that mean trick on you is probably hiding in the loft right now. Please go and look," she begged Billy's father.

He laughed. "Ary a soul would play a mean trick on us knowen we got a sick chile. You an' Granny Smith jist thought you seed somethen." He turned impatiently and strode back into the house.

"Will you let me search the loft?" Cherry asked his wife. "I'm sure someone is hiding there."

Mrs. Carter smiled faintly. "Iffen Ezekiel had-a felt the barn needed sarchen he'd-a done hit himself. Thank you kindly, though."

Granny Smith sniffed. "Hain't nobody in the loft. 'Twas Satan, Cherry. He peered right in the window where I was sleepen."

Cherry sighed and started down the hill. It was almost midnight when she reached the Whites' shack. The house was quiet and dark, and since she had passed no one on the way she concluded that Pansy and her baby were inside. And then she began to worry for fear the woman had climbed down the hill to the spring before Cherry had climbed up it. If so, it was too late now to prevent the baby from being dipped in the icy water.

She sank down on the sagging porch step, tired and depressed. Everything suddenly seemed hopeless. Little Jon would probably develop pneumonia, and Lu— She didn't dare think about Lu and the possibility of a ruptured appendix.

Granny Smith, convinced that the devil had put a curse on the money, would never agree to a truce. The man who had rigged up the frightening contraption with the aid of the Carters' clothesline had done it in order to make sure that Granny Smith would not interfere with his plans.

Whether he had come to the valley for the purpose of buying the Clarke-Smith land, or for the purpose of finding the long-lost money, Cherry couldn't know. But either way, the success of his plan depended on the families being in a state of war. And *that* meant that the two grannies must be kept in a state of terror.

Mr. Chase Spofford was staying with the Clarkes, so he could easily have found out that Granny Smith, since the rain began Wednesday afternoon, had been occupying his former room at the Carters', next door. The clothesline pulley, plus the missing basketball, had made it all too easy.

Cherry remembered that when she had examined the artists' supplies in the mule train Tuesday night she had been tempted to buy the children a tube of luminescent paint. But since it was rather expensive, she had finally decided to wait until the next trip. Mr. Spofford, she felt sure, *had* bought a tube, in order to eke out his supply of ghostly props.

Gossip traveled fast in this small community. Mingling most of the night with the crowd around the half-track, he had probably heard that the two old cronies had been hobnobbing together that very afternoon. He had undoubtedly made up his mind to stop the fraternizing as soon as possible.

He didn't have to buy a head for his flying "devil," because when Bertha asked him to put up the barrel hoop she had told him that there was a basketball in the school supply box. He must have stolen it while all the children, except Lu, were eating in the community loom house. Then he had painted on the missing basketball a face with eyes and a mouth that would glow in the dark.

The rain had delayed his plan for frightening Granny Smith until tonight. And, if he had not already done so, he soon would do something to terrorize Granny Clarke. That would be easy, too, since he was living in the same house with her. As long as the reign of terror lasted, there could be no hope for a truce and Bruce and Eliza would not be allowed to marry each other.

Cherry walked slowly along the bypath to the hillside road. It was now twenty minutes after midnight. Apparently Pansy had not taken Jon to the spring after all. If she had, she would have returned by now. The fact that she must have somehow conquered her superstitions was encouraging.

Cherry began to feel more hopeful. Slowly but surely the mothers of all the babies were beginning to follow young Mrs. Powell's shining example. If only the older women could be won over to modern medicine as easily! Cherry was worried most of all about Lu's mother. She might stubbornly refuse to let Dr. Jessup operate if he decided it was necessary.

But there was no sense in crossing that bridge until they came to it. The long hours between now and the doctor's arrival must somehow be got through.

CHAPTER X

The Missing Basketball

CHERRY THOUGHT SHE HAD NEVER HEARD A MORE WEL-come sound than the roar of Dr. Jessup's helicopter. She was in the muddy pasture waiting for him when he landed. He took one look at her white, drawn face and said:

"Good heavens! One week in Heartbreak Hollow has robbed you of your rosy cheeks! What's happened?"

She told him as they hurried toward the clinic. "Bertha and I feel pretty sure you'll want to fly Lu right back to the Titusville Hospital," she said. "But you're going to have trouble with her mother. She's with Lu now and is bound and determined to give her sulphur and molasses."

The handsome young doctor frowned. "That," he said grimly, "would be murder. And I'll tell her that in so many words if I have to. I've found that you have to be firm with Mrs. Clarke, and that the best way to handle her is to move so fast that she doesn't know what's happening until after it's all over."

Cherry never knew exactly how Dr. Jessup achieved what to her had seemed the impossible. But half an hour after he had examined Lu, the matter was settled. Mrs. Clarke had not only consented to the operation but had decided to accompany Lu to the hospital.

"I hain't a-feerd to fly in that thar contraption," she said defiantly as she marched beside Dr. Jessup, who was carrying Lu in his arms.

"Good for you," he said approvingly. "My mother will enjoy having you spend the week with her. You can visit Lu twice a day in the hospital. By this time tomorrow she'll be up and out of bed. You'll be glad to get rid of that useless little appendix, won't you, Lu?"

The child smiled weakly, but she was obviously not at all afraid. Eliza came running up then with the bundle of clothes she had packed for them both. Her father, who had remained stoically calm throughout the proceedings, helped Dr. Jessup place Lu on the stretcher he had hooked across the two rear seats. A few minutes later the helicopter was flying high above the hills. It had all happened so quickly that Cherry could hardly believe it.

And then Eliza threw her arms around her father's neck and burst into tears. "Lu ain't never comen back," she sobbed hysterically. "An' hit's all my fault fer courten with Bruce. Iffen I had never laid eyes on him, Lu would never have took sick. I hate him, Paw, I do!"

Cherry's shoulders slumped tiredly. Granny Clarke

was, of course, the cause of Eliza's hysteria. And she had a whole week until Lu's return to make matters worse. If only Eliza could have gone to the hospital with Lu and seen how rapidly children nowadays recover from operations! But there was nothing anyone could do between now and the doctor's next visit to convince Eliza that her little sister was not going to die.

A week of suspense, goaded by her granny, might well turn Eliza's love for Bruce to hate. Something had to be done. And then Cherry had an idea. When the girl's sobs finally subsided, she said:

"Eliza, honey, I wish you'd let me stay with you while Lu and your mother are away. It's lonely at the clinic now that Bertha has moved to the school. I promise not to be any trouble, and I could help you keep house if you'd let me."

Josh Clarke smiled gratefully at Cherry. "You'd shorely be mighty welcome, Miss Cherry. Granny is taken on somethen fierce about Lu. She hadn't oughta blame hit on Eliza." He cupped his daughter's chin in his big, work-worn hand. "Stop your fretten, chile," he said tenderly. "Lu hain't a-goen to die. The doctor's a mighty knowen man an' he tole me hisself that she wan't. He hain't never lied to none o' us yit about nothen."

As he talked Eliza began to cheer up a little. Shyly she said to Cherry, "Hit would be a pure delight iffen you'd stay with us. Maybe Paw would kindly wagon

Lu's bed back home so's you could sleep along with me in the same room."

"Shore I will," her father said soothingly. "Hit's been mighty lonesome fer you, Eliza, since Lu moved down to the school. I never did see two sisters," he told Cherry, "so 'tached one to t'other." He chuckled. "When Eliza gits married she'll have to take Lu along with her to her new home."

"I'll never git married," Eliza cried fiercely. "Never."

"Maybe not to Bruce," her father said quietly. "I don't aim to let a gal o' mine marry a critter that'd pizen another's hog."

At that, Eliza burst into tears again. "Bruce didn't do hit, Paw," she wailed. "Even Granny says so now. Hit was the devil. I seed him myself this mornen."

"Don't talk so flighty," he said rather sternly. "You bin to school, chile. You know there hain't no devil 'cepten in Granny's mind."

"But I seed him," Eliza insisted. "I couldn't seem to sleep nohow las' night, a-worryen about Lu. Come mornen, whilst the chillun was still sleepen, I went to the woods fer some kindlen so I could build a fire an' warm up the schoolhouse." She shuddered reminiscently. " 'Twas then I seed him, a-comen down the path from Smiths', a shovel over one shoulder." Her voice rose to an hysterical pitch. "A-diggen Lu's grave he was!"

Cherry herself had not slept a wink the night before, and the long hours of anxious waiting until the doctor's arrival had worn her nerves thin. "You didn't see any devil," she told Eliza sharply. "What you saw was a flesh-and-blood man who spends all the time he can digging in the old tobacco field. He's trying to find the money that belongs to you and the Smiths." She turned to Josh Clarke. "And if you don't watch out, he'll find it. Oh, why can't you people stop your silly feuding? If you'd only call a truce for a few days and work together plowing that land—" She stopped, ashamed of herself for losing her temper. "I'm sorry," she finished meekly. "It's none of my business, Mr. Clarke. Please forgive me."

Instead of showing anger, he combed his curly black beard with his hand and asked her quietly, "Who do you suspicion, Miss Cherry? Ary a soul in this valley would put foot on that land without the say-so of us Clarkes an' the Smiths."

Again Cherry's temper flared up. "Don't tell me *you* believe in the devil, Mr. Clarke," she cried.

"Course not," he said easily. "But 'pears like I cain't believe neither that a body who'd accept my hospitality would go an' do some trespassen."

"Well, *I* can believe it," Cherry said. "Anybody who would poison your hog and ruin the Smiths' wool wouldn't let the rules of hospitality interfere with his evil plans." She went on in a calmer voice, "You're thinking of the same person I am, aren't you, Mr. Clarke?"

He shrugged. "I aim to study on what you bin sayen,

Miss Cherry." He walked slowly away then, his hands thrust in his pockets, his broad shoulders bent.

Eliza stared after him, her round eyes wide with amazement. "Mr. Spofford," she gasped. "You suspicion that hit was him I seed this mornen?"

Cherry nodded. "But I haven't any proof, Eliza." She told her then all the reasons why she had suspected the "city feller" from the very beginning. "Who else," she asked, "has any reason for wanting your two families to hate each other?"

"Ary a soul," Eliza replied promptly. "The very idee o' him maken out like hit was my Bruce who pizened our hog!" She clenched her hands into small fists. "I'll git the proof fer you, Cherry. I'll git hit this very mornen when I right up his room!"

Cherry could hardly believe her ears. At midnight when she had been sitting disconsolately on the Whites' sagging step she had thought everything was hopeless. And now Lu was safely on her way to a hospital, and Eliza and Josh Clarke were proving themselves not to be as superstition-ridden as she had thought they were.

Furthermore, during his short stay in the hollow, Dr. Jessup had found time to put his official stamp of approval on the isolation ward. Cherry had quickly rounded up the parents of the "boarding school" children before his departure. Using the magic word "school," he had convinced them that now each child must receive his whooping cough, diphtheria, and tetanus shots.

Bertha was at this very moment waiting for Cherry so they could launch the immunization program. Eliza, now that she had recovered from her hysteria, would want to help, too. Finding the proof of Mr. Spofford's guilt could wait, Cherry decided.

"After we've given the children their shots," she told Eliza, "I'll help you tidy up your house. Together we ought to find something which will convince your father that Spofford's the devil."

Right after lunch she and Eliza went into the guest room, armed with brooms and mops. But although they turned the mattress on the bed and took everything out of the cupboards, they found no sign of the missing ties, the red flannels, and basketball. Eliza's suspicions of Mr. Spofford were already on the wane. Throughout the noon meal Granny Clarke had talked of nothing but Lu, who, in her opinion, had taken a short cut to heaven via the helicopter.

Josh Clarke had eaten in a moody silence. Mr. Spofford was not there, for, according to Eliza, he never arose before eleven and usually combined lunch with breakfast then. Sleeping so late in itself was suspicious, Cherry had said for the benefit of Mr. Clarke. People who went to bed early and stayed there all night usually got up early, didn't they? Josh gave no indication that he had heard Cherry's remarks. And neither did Eliza.

After they had virtually taken the guest room apart, she said to Cherry, " 'Pears like we was wrong to suspicion him. I reckon the wind blowed Mr. Carter's flannels offen the line, an' Billy, he did swipe them ties. Billy was allus a-borrowen things from Miss Scope when she stayed at Carters'. He's jist a leetle boy an' don't mean no harm."

"Well, he didn't borrow the basketball," Cherry pointed out patiently. "He hasn't left the house since a week ago today."

And then Mrs. Carter suddenly appeared on the Clarkes' front porch with the missing ball in the crook of her arm. She handed it to Cherry and said with a puzzled frown, "Found this under Billy's bed jist now. Who do you reckon put it thar?"

The ball was suspiciously clean and smelled strongly of turpentine. Cherry's temper flared. If the man thought he was going to shift the blame for his petty thievery to a boy, he had another think coming. Mr. Spofford was undoubtedly counting on the fact that Billy was the type of little patient who always gets out of bed whenever he is left alone. But that was stupid of him, for although Billy probably did scamper around his room whenever he could, he could not possibly have gone down to the schoolhouse and back without being missed or seen on the way by someone.

"Mr. Spofford," she asked Mrs. Carter, "stopped in to see Billy this morning, didn't he?"

The tired-looking little woman shook her head.

"Maybe he did when you were out of the house," Cherry persisted.

Again Mrs. Carter shook her head. "When I was

holpen Zeke plant corn, Granny Smith she set with Billy an' he didn't say nothen about seein' Mr. Spofford."

"But Granny Smith went home at eleven thirty," Cherry pointed out. "I passed her going down the hill when I was coming up here. You and your husband were out in the field then."

Mrs. Carter looked surprised. "I tuck hit fer granted that she set with Billy till noon like she promised. It was jist a leetle atter twelve when I come home an' Billy was a-sleepen. I reckon he fell asleep about eleven an' Granny got the idee of taken off fer home a mite early."

"Then," Cherry went on, "Mr. Spofford could have gone to see Billy without anyone, not even Billy knowing it." She turned to Eliza. "Did you notice when he left the house this morning whether he went up the hill or down it?"

Eliza thought for a minute. "I got home about eleven. He was eaten then, I ricollect. Atter that he went into his room an' I didn't see him no more."

"Then," Cherry said, "he left the house by the door in his room which opens onto the back yard. Does he usually do that?"

"No," Eliza said. "He ginerally goes out by the front door. Hit's the nighest way to git to the road."

"That's right," Cherry said. "And the reason why he didn't leave by the front door this morning was because he was carrying something he didn't want you or your granny to see. Mrs. Carter," she went on, "you asked me who I thought put this ball under Billy's bed. I think Mr. Spofford did. I think he stole it from the schoolhouse and painted a scary face on it. Then, with the help of your husband's missing red flannels, stuffed with straw, he rigged up a dummy and attached it to your clothesline. That dummy was the frightening thing Granny Smith and I saw last night. I still feel sure that if your husband had searched the loft he would have found Mr. Spofford hiding there!"

Mrs. Carter sagged against the porch railing. "Never did like that city feller," she mumbled. "Him an' his hair smellen o' scented grease! The wind didn't blow away Zeke's red flannels, hit didn't. I had 'em 'tached to the line real good with them cloespins Miss Scope give me fer a present afore she tuck off las' fall."

"Hit was mighty windy Monday mornen," Eliza said doubtfully.

"I know it," Cherry said, trying to control her impatience. If Billy's mother suspected Mr. Spofford she would certainly discuss the matter with her husband. Ezekiel might then quite naturally gossip with his next-door neighbor, Josh Clarke, who was already mildly suspicious. In that case, it wouldn't be long before one or both of the men would decide to stay awake at night and determine whether or not Mr. Spofford remained in his room.

Cherry could see no hope of a truce, but there was a faint hope that Mr. Spofford might be caught in the act as he sneaked out the back door, garbed in the missing red flannel underwear. "I know it was windy Monday morning," she said to Eliza. "But don't you think it's queer that the only thing missing in Mrs. Carter's wash was something which would make a perfect devil's costume?"

"The devil?" Mrs. Carter repeated, her eyes wide with surprise. "Billy he keeps sayen he seed the devil in his red duds t'other night a-sneaken down the hill. I figgered hit was the fever a-burnen in him, Miss Cherry."

"Billy has never had enough fever to make him imagine things," Cherry said quietly. "What he saw was Mr. Spofford, *I* think, wearing your husband's missing red flannels!" She could tell by the gleam in the tired little woman's eyes that she could hardly wait to have a talk with her husband, who had undoubtedly scolded her roundly for losing those red flannels.

"Iffen you-all will 'scuse me," Mrs. Carter said, darting down the steps, "I'd shore like to ponder on this hyar sitiashun along with Zeke." She scurried off along the path that led down to the field where her husband was plowing.

Cherry called after her, "I'll sit with Billy until you come back." Then she said to Eliza, "I think we ought to search every room in your house. Why don't we give it a spring cleaning this afternoon? It would be a nice surprise for your mother when she comes back next Saturday with Lu."

"Lu hain't never comen back," Eliza said dolefully. "I feel hit in my bones that she is daid."

"Well, she isn't," Cherry said rather sharply. "While I'm sitting with Billy, won't you at least try to find those red flannels?"

With a sudden burst of sympathy, she put her arms around the young girl's thin shoulders and hugged her. "Please believe me, honey," she begged. "Lu *is* all right. And you and Bruce had nothing to do with her illness."

"I hate him, I do," Eliza sobbed. "I *hate* him!"

And then they both heard the sound of a deep, masculine voice singing the chorus of Stephen Foster's famous folk song:

"Weep no more, my lady,
Weep no more today,
We will sing one song
For my old Kentucky home,
For my old Kentucky home far a-way!"

"The minstrel," Eliza cried, tearing herself away from Cherry. "The minstrel, Granny," she shouted. "Jeremiah is a-comen up the road right now. Cain't we ask him to stay with us 'stid o' at Carters', Billy bein' sick an' all?"

The little old lady hastily joined them on the porch, chattering excitedly. "Course he's a-goen to visit with us, chile," she said. "Your paw kin put your maw's bed alongside o' Mr. Spofford's in the spare room jist as easy as scat."

Cherry smiled at the tall, freckle-faced young man

who was striding into the Clarkes' yard, singing at the top of his lungs as he strummed the accompaniment on his guitar.

"You don't know how welcome you are, Mr. Jeremiah Minstrel," she told him silently. "You've already cheered up Eliza, and, what's more, as long as you're sharing the guest room with Mr. Spofford, he won't dare do any 'traipsen' at night!"

CHAPTER XI

Jeremiah, the Minstrel

DURING THE MINSTREL'S STAY IN HEARTBREAK HOLLOW, Cherry and Eliza had no opportunity to search the house. The huge living room was filled with people from early in the morning to late at night. With the exception of the Clarke-Smith field, all the land had been plowed and planted by Saturday evening, and the men felt that they deserved a well-earned holiday.

The big house overflowed with men, women, and children who came to sing and dance or play in the orchestra. Granny Clarke, in spite of the fact that she had maintained Lu would die, gave no signs of going into mourning. When she wasn't dancing one of the old reels or singing lustily, she played on her dulcimer. She would lay the ancient instrument across her bony knees and triumphantly pick out a tune with two quills. It sounded like the whine of thousands of hungry mosquitoes to Cherry, but the other guests seemed to enjoy Granny Clarke's solos thoroughly.

As Cherry watched her, she couldn't help suspecting that the little old lady was not really worried about Lu. Had she simply taken advantage of the child's illness in order to keep Eliza under her thumb? The Clarke matriarch, Cherry decided, would allow nothing to stand in the path of her tyrannical rule. Her great-granddaughter had disobeyed her. Therefore, no punishment was too severe.

Granny Smith, although equally tyrannical, was much more humane. The Smiths, of course, never joined in the merrymaking at the Clarkes', and during the minstrel's visit, Cherry spent most of her spare time with old Mrs. Smith, who bitterly resented the fact that she hadn't "cotched Jeremiah fust." The fact that they could not share in the week's festivities served to increase Lincoln Smith's hostile attitude toward the Clarkes.

He and Bruce doggedly worked around the place, mending fences, painting, and doing odd repair jobs to the house. They greeted her warmly whenever she came to call, but gave her no opportunity to talk with them as she had to Eliza's father on Saturday.

"It probably wouldn't do any good, anyway," she told Bertha Wednesday evening. "I don't think Josh Clarke remembers now that he promised to 'study on' my suspicions of his house guest."

"You can't tell about that," Bertha said optimistically. "The people here move and think slowly, but they don't forget easily. Have you made any progress with Granny Smith?"

"None at all," Cherry admitted ruefully. "She flatly refuses to discuss the devil with me in any form. Sometimes I think she knows more than I do. She acts so sly and secretive whenever I mention Mr. Spofford's name. And she pretended she didn't hear me when I told her Mrs. Carter had found the missing basketball under Billy's bed. I came right out and asked her if Mr. Spofford had been visiting Billy when she left Saturday morning. Do you know what she said?"

"I can guess." Bertha chuckled. "*She* came right out and told you to mind your own business."

"That's right." Cherry laughed. "Anyway, to change the subject as she does whenever it suits her fancy, I have good news for you. Jerry the minstrel is going to leave Friday evening, but he promised to spend all of that day down here with the children. He's going to have a singing school, he says, and told me to invite the Smiths. He's very fond of them, you know, and was awfully sorry to hear that the feud had flared up."

Bertha's china-blue eyes twinkled mischievously. "I suppose since you've had such a heart-to-heart talk with our Jeremiah you haven't kept him in the dark as to your feelings concerning Mr. Spofford?"

Cherry flushed. "Someday I guess I'll be sued for libel, but I'll bet it won't be by that Spofford man. And Jerry sees eye-to-eye with me. He keeps saying he's sure he has seen Mr. Spofford somewhere else, but the name is not at all familiar."

"He might have seen him at a broadcasting station in

New York," Bertha said easily. "During the winter, Jerry sings hillbilly songs over the radio, you know."

Cherry nodded. "I think that young man will end up in Hollywood. He's got a beautiful voice. When you talked about a minstrel, I expected to see an old man with a long, white beard, riding on a mule. Not an attractive young man who, he tells me, travels over the mountains in a jeep."

Bertha giggled. "The jeep is something new. I was surprised myself when Jerry appeared in it last Saturday. And his father, from whom Jerry inherited his profession, *was* an old man with a long, white beard. He rode astride a mule, Granny Clarke told me. He retired long before my time. I think Jerry carries on just to please his father, don't you? He could make a lot of money singing all the year around on the radio."

"No," Cherry said thoughtfully. "I think Jerry carries on because he loves these people and their ballads and traditions. He admires their serenity, independence, and dignity. I wish Mr. Spofford appreciated Heartbreak Hollow the way Jerry does." She shuddered. "That man hates me, Bertha. Every now and then during the parties up on the hill I would suddenly find him staring at me with daggers in his eyes. I think he knows I suspect him."

Bertha frowned. "In that case, Cherry, you must be careful. Don't you go wandering around alone at night. If anybody is sick and sends for you after dark, get Josh Clarke to go with you." She stared thoughtfully at her injured ankle. "I'm going to have a long talk with Frank on Saturday and tell him that I really think he ought to check up on our 'city feller.' If it hadn't been for Lu, I would have discussed your suspicions with him last week."

"So," Cherry said, with a laugh, "you don't think we need proof any more? At first you said—"

"I know," Bertha interrupted, "but that basketball smelling of turpentine is concrete evidence enough for me. Plus the fact that it was found under the bed of Billy Carter, who couldn't possibly have swiped it. Not to mention the fact that nobody else in this hollow would take anything from the school. Why, it's almost as sacred as their church." She glanced up at the Carters' house on the hill. "I suppose Mr. Spofford felt sure that not even you could keep a Heartbreak Hollow child in quarantine, and since Billy reacted so quickly to chloromycetin, I imagine it never occurred to our 'devil' that your way of keeping him in quarantine was to keep him in bed."

"It seemed to me," Cherry said, "the only way to make sure he didn't catch cold, especially during the rainy days. And since Jerry the Minstrel arrived, all the mothers have been bringing their babies right next door for the singing. Anyway," she went on, "Friday, while Jerry is conducting his singing school down here, I'm going to search the Clarke house from top to bottom. That is, if Eliza will let me."

"Why should she object?" Bertha asked. "Don't tell

me she still thinks the devil stuck his pitchfork into Lu's side?"

"I don't know what she thinks," Cherry said disconsolately. "But she certainly can't think her granny believes Lu is dead. Why, that woman has been having the time of her life ever since Jerry arrived!" She giggled and then sobered. "I haven't had a chance to talk with Eliza. She's busy all day cooking and cleaning up after the guests. I go to sleep at night while the merrymaking is still in full swing."

"I don't know how you can sleep through the noise," Bertha said. "I can hear it down here until the wee, sma' hours."

"It's my early training," Cherry said. "Before Charlie went away to college he used to keep his radio blaring most of the night. Mother, Dad, and I all learned to sleep through it. So did Charlie. He used to fall asleep in the middle of a program, and so the darn thing would keep going until the first person who woke up in the morning turned it off." She resolutely swallowed the lump of homesickness that was rising in her throat. "I hope Dr. Jessup brings me some letters from home on Saturday."

"He will," Bertha assured her. "And let's hope we get good news from Mai Lee then, too. She's had plenty of time to show those samples to several stores. Didn't you say she was on night duty?"

Cherry nodded. "And no matter what her hours are, Mai Lee always gets up early in the morning, you know.

I don't dare think about what the verdict will be!"

"I can't bear to think of these people being disappointed," Bertha agreed. "Let's not worry. I'm sure Mai Lee will report success."

Cherry turned and saw the young minstrel striding along the road from the loom house. He called out to her:

"I was hoping you'd let me accompany you on your rounds. I'm no good at nursing, but I could carry your bag."

"Fine," she said, smiling. "I was just about to take Billy Carter for a little walk. It would cheer him up a lot if you'd sing a few ballads and strum on your guitar."

Jerry took her satchel and said, frowning, "I should have thought of that long ago. The poor kid! I remember, his favorite song is one about a miner who—" He stopped, clutching his curly blond hair. "That's it. Now I know where I saw your Mr. Chase Spofford before!"

Bertha had already hobbled into the schoolhouse, from which now came the sounds of children's voices. In another minute they would be dashing out on the porch. Once they caught sight of the young minstrel they would be in no mood for the three R's.

Cherry grabbed his arm. "Come on," she said. "We've got to run until we're out of sight." They raced along the rutted road and didn't stop until they were halfway up the hill. Then Cherry gasped, "Tell me quickly. I can't stand it another second. Where did you see Mr. Spofford before?"

CHAPTER XII

Jerry's Scheme

"MY LUNGS ARE BURSTING," JERRY GROANED. "ANOTHER mad dash like that and my singing career is over!"

Cherry giggled. "Don't be silly. Anyone who can sing for hours on end the way you do could run right up to the top of Old Desolate without stopping. Please answer my question! Where did you see Mr. Spofford before?"

He sobered. "On the other side of Old Desolate. In a mining town. He ran a gambling house until he was politely given the choice between leaving under his own steam or on a rail after being tarred and feathered. And," he went on, "unless I'm badly mistaken, his name then wasn't Chase Spofford. It was Spud Chaseman."

"*Could* you be mistaken?" Cherry asked. "I mean, are you sure enough to accuse him of having changed his name?"

"No, I'm not," he admitted ruefully. "I was only a kid when I saw him last. The mine was abandoned two or three years ago, and he galloped away in the dead of night about four years before that. I could swear to *you* that he's Spud Chaseman, but not in a court of law. His hair was as sandy as mine then, not black the way it is now, but he slicked it down with the same unpleasant goo. I remember hating the smell of it. Teen-age kids are sensitive to that kind of thing, you know. It permeated the whole hall where Dad used to sing."

"If it hadn't been for that pomade," Cherry said thoughtfully, "you might never have recognized him."

"That's right," he agreed as they started on up the hill. "Smells, like old songs, usually bring back haunting memories. The first night I shared the Clarkes' guest room with him, I dreamed of that old mining town. I thought it was because it was there that I first heard the story of the Clarke-Smith feud. It both fascinated and saddened me, especially after I'd met Bruce and Eliza. Dad's a preacher, you know, and although he's retired, he counted on officiating at their wedding. He worked for years trying to bring the two families together, but no go, until Dr. Jessup arrived."

"Your father will perform that ceremony yet," Cherry said firmly. "That Spud Spofford man ought not to escape being tarred and feathered this time."

"Two wrongs never make a right, my dear girl," he said.

"I know," Cherry agreed in a mollified tone of voice. "But in his case I'd like to follow the old eye-for-an-eye rule. He's caused so much unhappiness here!"

He sighed. "And there's absolutely nothing we can do about it. I can't be positively sure that he's Spud Chaseman, and you can't really prove any of your suspicions. Even if you found his devil's outfit, you couldn't pin it on him."

"I could," Cherry said defiantly, "if I caught him in it. And that is just about what I've decided to do."

He stared at her unbelievingly. "Do you mean to imply that you're going to haunt that gravedigger one moonlight night? Why, if he's what we think he is, he wouldn't hesitate to bash you over the head with his shovel!" He stopped. "Promise me right now, on your word of honor, that you won't do anything foolish after I've gone."

Cherry hesitated. She knew that the person who was masquerading as the devil was ruthless, and that spying on his activities at night would be dangerous and probably foolhardy. But, on the other hand, something had to be done to stop him before it was too late. She felt quite sure that he would do no ghostly digging as long as Jerry was in the hollow, sharing the same room with him. Jerry would leave day after tomorrow in the early part of the evening. Spofford, she sensed, guessed that she suspected him. Fearing that she might report her suspicions to Dr. Jessup on Saturday, wouldn't he resume his search for the money as soon as it was safe on Friday night? Suppose he found it? Wouldn't he again "gallop away in the dead of night"?

"We mustn't let him," she said out loud. "That man must have heard about the feud in the mining town where you heard about it, Jerry. He's probably been planning for years to come back to this area and search for that money. It wouldn't take a very brilliant mind to figure out that it's buried in the field that hasn't been plowed since the feud began. Even *I* figured that out."

"I know," he said soberly, "but you can't risk your life trying to prove your suspicions. I agree with you that the money is probably buried in the old tobacco field. But I doubt if Spud Spofford is going to find it in a hurry. The wise thing for you to do is to keep hammering at the Clarkes and the Smiths to call a truce. I'll have a talk with all four men myself before I leave. Working together they could find the money in less than a day—if it's there."

Cherry sighed. "All right, you talk to them. I've talked myself hoarse and have got nowhere fast."

He frowned down at her. "Promise me that you'll stick to your nursing? No sleuthing?"

"I won't promise not to sleuth," Cherry said. "But I will promise not to do anything silly."

He shook his head. "I've got to be satisfied with that, I suppose." They trudged on in silence until they arrived at the Carters' home.

Billy's temperature, Cherry made sure, was still normal. He was feeling much too well to be kept in bed all day. His mother looked as though her patience had been exhausted. Cherry left the boy chatting gaily with the young minstrel and drew Mrs. Carter into the living room.

"Billy," she said, "on these fine days, can be up and around if he is warmly dressed and can be kept quiet. Now that he has stopped vomiting, he can go back on a fairly normal diet. Three or four light meals a day—nothing indigestible, of course. I thought it might be easier for you if he followed you around while you do your housework. But, in order to be sure that he doesn't get overtired or overheated or come in contact with other children, you must keep your eye on him constantly. Do you think you can do that, or should I send Eliza to help?"

"Eliza," Mrs. Carter said with a smile, "hain't got no time to holp me. Don't you fret, Cherry, Billy an' me will get along real nicely. I'd be mighty grateful iffen you'd drap in fer a leetle twicet a day to pleasure him. I don't hardly dairst let him out o' the house 'thout you. Likely as not, he'd go a-traipsen down to the schoolhouse. He's that lonesome, he is."

"I know he is," Cherry cried sympathetically. "All the boys his own age are down there. If only one of them had already had whooping cough—"

"Brian Hopkins had hit," Mrs. Carter said slyly. "His maw called hit the chin cough, but hit was the same thing Billy cotched."

Cherry stared at her, torn between surprise and impatience. "But I don't understand," she said. "If Brian had it, why didn't his mother tell me or Dr. Jessup?"

Mrs. Carter shrugged. "Likely as not you never axed her iffen he had the *chin* cough. Mary Hopkins, she aims fer Brian to git all the larnen he can git. He's a mighty troublesome young 'un when he hain't got nothen to do with hisself." She lowered her voice to a gossipy whisper. "My Zeke thinks hit was Brian who rigged up that contraption that scairt Granny Smith t'other night."

"That's impossible," Cherry said emphatically. "Bertha would have known if Brian had left the schoolhouse. Besides, even though he *is* a mischievous little boy, he wouldn't have thought of such a mean trick."

Again Mrs. Carter shrugged. "I'm jist a-tellen you what Zeke an' Josh Clarke says to me when I told 'em who you suspicioned."

Jerry came out of the bedroom then, carrying Billy in his arms. "We're dressed warmly," Jerry said to Cherry, "except for the feet. Is it all right for your patient to go barefoot?"

Cherry nodded. "It's all right now when the sun is shining so warmly. But I think he ought to have something on his feet, Mrs. Carter, in the early morning and in the evening when it's damp and cold."

Mrs. Carter laughed. "The toes of his shoes is busted out but he can still wear 'em."

"I won't," Billy announced, squirming down to the floor. "I'll tie my foots up in rags fust."

"That's a good idea," Cherry said placatingly. "Then your toes will be as warm as your heels. You don't want to catch cold, Billy. If you have even a tiny sniffle you'll have to stay in bed all day long again. But if you're very good and mind your mother you won't have to stay in bed after this except for a nap after lunch."

Billy was as docile as a lamb during his short walk with Cherry and Jerry. Then they sat on the porch while Jerry sang and strummed on his guitar. Cherry stayed with the Carters until it was time for supper at the Clarkes'. When she arrived, Mr. Spofford was helping Eliza serve the guests with plates heaped high with delicious-smelling food. Jerry was presiding over the huge ham which had already dwindled to half its size.

He beckoned to her with his carving knife. "Come over here by the fire, you northerner," he called, "and take a look at ham as it should be." When she came close, he added in a low voice, "I've got a plan which may or may not work. As soon as everyone has scraped his plate clean, I'll sing a little ditty which I just made up. While I'm singing, you watch Mr. Spofford's face."

"Don't be so mysterious," Cherry begged. "What song—?"

"Red-brown, not pink," he interrupted loudly. "That's the proper color for ham." And he did not speak to her again until even the last sleepy child had finished everything on his plate.

Then he suddenly burst into song:

"Clap your hands,
Stamp your feet.

Have you had enough to eat?
If you haven't
Chew your cud,
Or better still,
Go eat a—SPUD!"

He shouted the last word in such a loud voice that even Cherry jumped. Mr. Spofford, who had not been listening to the song, did more than jump. He leaped to his feet and whirled around to face the young minstrel.

Jerry went right on singing as though nothing had happened.

"Some calls 'em taters,
Some calls 'em spuds,
Some calls 'em clothes,
Some calls 'em duds.
So clap your hands,
Stamp your feet—"

By that time everyone, except Mr. Spofford, was stamping and clapping. The rest of the words to Jerry's song were drowned out when Granny Clarke began picking out the tune on her dulcimer. Not until then did Mr. Spofford stop staring at Jerry. To Cherry he looked as though he had been hypnotized, and even when he began clapping and stamping, his heart was obviously not in it.

Later, when the orchestra was in full sway, Jerry

danced Cherry out on the porch. The moon, although no longer full, was shining brightly.

"That did it," he told her. "He's Spud Chaseman all right. And what's more, I think he recognizes me as the singing-parson's freckle-faced boy."

"I think so, too," Cherry agreed. "And I think he's badly frightened. Maybe he'll leave this very night."

Jerry nodded. "That was my idea. Without proof I can't very well accuse him of being here under false pretenses. But I thought if he guessed I knew all about his unsavory background, he'd depart hurriedly."

"I hope he does," Cherry said. But to herself she added, "Ten thousand dollars is an awful lot of money. And since he isn't really doing anything illegal except trespass, why should he be afraid?"

CHAPTER XIII

Dr. Jessup Is Worried

AS IT TURNED OUT, MR. SPOFFORD WAS STILL THERE ON Saturday morning when Dr. Jessup arrived with a very much alive Lucretza. Everyone in the community who could gathered in the pasture to witness her safe return. She and her mother had to relate their experiences over and over again.

Mrs. Clarke took off her shoes the minute she stepped out of the helicopter. "I declare," she told her husband, "the blisters on my feet bothered me a sight more than the knife did Lu." She turned to her grandmother-in-law and said sternly, "I don't never want to hear no more talk about the devil an' his pitchfork. Hear?"

Granny Clarke sucked in her lips angrily. "Getten above yourself sence you been on the outside, hain't you?"

Lu's mother ignored her and took Eliza into her arms. "Honey," she said tenderly, "I knowed you thought you was to blame fer Lu's pains, but you wan't. Hit was a little ol' thing no bigger than a fat worm. I seed one in a bottle at the hospital." She hugged Eliza and said to her husband with surprising defiance in her voice, "Josh, I did a spell o' thinken whilst I was on the outside. In my jedgment, neither Bruce nor his paw pizened our hog. Hit was most likely an accident."

"Accident," the old granny snorted. "Hit was the devil."

Mrs. Clarke whirled on her. "Granny," she said slowly, "I'm mighty proud to have you stay with us, but I don't aim to put up with no more sech talk." She appealed to her husband. "You tell her, Josh. We cain't have our gals scairt out o' their wits by her foolishness."

Cherry held her breath and guessed that everyone who had gathered around the helicopter was as excited as she was. Even Dr. Jessup stood quietly waiting for Josh's reply.

"Well, now," he said at last, "you womenfolks has got to live together peaceable. 'Pears like Granny can think about the devil if she has a mind to, long as she keeps her thoughts to herself."

Lu, who had been clinging fondly to his arm, spoke up then. "Paw, you got to let Eliza marry Bruce. You jist got to. Look at her, all pale an' peaked. She's fallen off somethen terrible sence I last seed her only a week ago."

"It's the truth," Dr. Jessup put in. "I could hardly believe it when Lu and her mother told me you believed the Smiths poisoned your hog, Josh. You know neither Lincoln nor Bruce would do such a thing. It must have been an accident." He frowned. "And what's all this I hear about someone ruining the Smiths' wool?"

To Cherry's surprise, Lincoln Smith, who had been standing on the outside of the crowd, spoke up then, his voice gruff. "That wan't no accident. Josh did hit an' his granny put him up to hit." He strode away then as silently as he had come.

Dr. Jessup picked up his big black satchel. "I've got work to do," he said shortly. "If you'd like to discuss this matter with me, Josh, come to the clinic around five."

With Cherry at his side he hurried across the pasture to the sloping road. Not until then did Cherry remember to ask him if he'd brought any mail.

"Why, yes," he replied, reaching into his coat pocket. "Two letters for you and one for Bertha. There's also a package for you in the helicopter. I forgot all about it."

"It doesn't matter," Cherry said. "I wouldn't dare open my mail until the clinic closes for the noon hour. I'd be so excited I wouldn't be much help."

"Expecting a letter from your beau?" he asked, teasing.

Cherry told him then that Bertha had written Mai Lee about the beautiful hand-woven things the Heartbreak Hollow people made and had sent her some samples on the mule train. "I didn't have a chance to tell you last Saturday," she finished. "Do you think we did the right thing?"

He nodded approvingly. "It's a splendid idea. I should have thought of it myself." He grinned. "And maybe you can wait until lunchtime to hear what your friend wrote Bertha, but I can't. I couldn't help noticing that the return address on the envelope is your famous No. 9. Take that letter to her at once and find out what the verdict is. That's an order."

Five minutes later Bertha was reading Mai Lee's letter to Cherry:

"I read your letter to my patient, who happens to be a very good friend of the buyer in the house-furnishing department of Simpson and Company, which, as you know, is one of the biggest Fifth Avenue stores. My patient promptly gave me a letter of introduction to Miss Jane Righter, who is one of the most charming people I've ever met. She is buying now for October displays, which is when Christmas shopping really begins, and was so interested in your idea that when the samples arrived she came right down to No. 9 to see them.

"Honestly, girls, she was wildly enthusiastic and wanted to buy the samples then and there. I am enclosing an itemized list of the prices she will pay for them and for reorders. She wants an exclusive on everything Heartbreak Hollow makes, and plans for the publicity and advertising departments to start a campaign right away. Will you let me know as soon as possible if her prices are satisfactory? If so, please send some snapshots of the people and the locale which would reproduce well in newspapers and magazines, and also as much as you can write about them, their customs, problems, etc. The two grannies sound like wonderful material. As soon as we hear from you, Jane Righter will send you a check for the samples which will amount to almost two hundred dollars."

Cherry didn't wait to hear the rest of the letter. Two hundred dollars just for the samples! It was too good to be true. With the price list in her hand she raced over to the clinic, where Dr. Jessup had just finished giving Jon White his physical exam.

"This youngster," he said, as he lifted the baby from the scales, "has picked up remarkably."

Pansy White, beaming proudly, took Jon from him and began to dress him. Cherry handed the price list to Dr. Jessup, and while he glanced through it, she washed her hands and went out on the porch to usher in Mrs. Hopkins and Betty.

Dr. Jessup glanced up from the list and said in an awed voice, "Wow! This calls for a meeting. Why, there must be several thousand dollars' worth of stuff over in the loom house." He stopped and stared in amazement at plump little Betty. "Can this be the Hopkins baby?" he demanded. "We'd better watch out," he said to the proud mother, "or she'll end up as the fat lady in the circus."

From then on, Cherry was kept busy filling in the blank spaces on the little patients' charts. Then the expectant mothers came in one by one to be weighed and have their blood pressure taken. Dr. Jessup gave them all envelopes containing a month's supply of iron and calcium tablets.

"They're all doing fine," he told Cherry as she filed the last chart. "Mrs. Sexton gained a little more than she should have, but since she was underweight to begin with, we won't worry. At this time of the year when the vegetables have only just been planted, I'm afraid she's existing solely on corn bread and sorghum. You might check up on all of them during the week to make sure they're taking their vitamins."

Cherry nodded. "I wish we had some extra vitamins to give to the Wilson children, Dr. Jessup. They look like they're suffering from malnutrition. If only there was some way we could arrange things so that they could have the leftovers which people like the Smiths and Clarkes feed to their pigs." She flushed. "That sounds awful, but I mean it."

"I know just what you mean," he said soberly. "But the Wilsons are too proud to accept 'table leavens.' "

"That's the trouble," Cherry admitted. "But I was just thinking that since we have a community loom house, why not a community canning kitchen? If families like the Wilsons helped put up in jars the surplus from all the gardens, they wouldn't object to eating the vegetables during the months when nothing is growing. Chickens, broths, soups and stews could be canned too. And why not a community milk bar where families who have no cows could buy the surplus from other farms for a few pennies a quart? Eggs, too, and—"

"You've got something there," he interrupted enthusiastically. "And the foundation for the whole idea is already set up in the way Bertha is running the isolation ward. All we have to do, actually, is enlarge that project. I'll suggest it at the meeting this afternoon." He chuckled. "Everyone is bound to be in a co-operative mood when they hear Mai Lee's good news."

Everyone *was* in a co-operative mood that afternoon. The cheers that followed Dr. Jessup's reading of the price list were deafening. Granny Smith was triumphant; one would have thought that she had arranged the whole thing. But in the end she made a little speech giving full credit to the two nurses. After that, Dr. Jessup's suggestion for a community canning kitchen and a milk bar was unanimously approved.

Then a committee of men took an inventory of the loom-house products, and, after comparing it with Mai Lee's price list, they announced in awed voices that the community could now afford to pay a teacher an extra hundred dollars a month.

"That's fine," Dr. Jessup said, "because Miss Scope got in touch with me the other day. She wants very much to come back. She couldn't stay on at the previous salary because she has to support an invalid sister who was injured in an automobile accident last fall."

"So that's why she quit," Bertha said. "I wondered because she seemed to love working here."

"I can fly her in next Saturday," Dr. Jessup said. "If there are no signs of a whooping cough epidemic by then, the children who have not yet had it need no longer be isolated. They may return to their homes, but I think that all the children should continue working in the school garden and they should continue having hot meals here in the loom-house kitchen."

Everyone agreed to that proposal and then the meeting broke up. At last Cherry and Bertha had a chance to discuss their suspicions of Chase Spofford with Dr. Jessup. He listened in silence until they had finished and then he said soberly, "I wish I'd known about this last week. But I suppose you didn't have a chance to tell me during the excitement of getting Lu off to the hospital. There's only one thing I can do. Check with the philanthropist he's supposed to be representing. Spofford can't very well refuse to divulge his name to me."

"But," Cherry wailed, "we're sure he isn't representing anyone. He made up that philanthropist in order to cover his real reason for coming here, which was to find the Clarke-Smith money."

He shrugged. "I agree with you, it certainly looks like that. But how can I accuse him without some proof?"

"The basketball—" Bertha began.

"The missing red flannels," Cherry put in.

He laughed. "Those clues don't impress me nearly as much as the 'accidents' that happened to the Clarkes' hog and the Smiths' wool." He glanced at his wrist watch. "I'll go up to the Clarkes' now. I've got just about time for a talk with Spofford and another one with Josh, if he'll listen."

"I'll go with you," Cherry said. "Now that Lu's home I must pack my things and move back to the clinic."

"I'd rather you wouldn't," Dr. Jessup said as they started off. "If that man is really a criminal you shouldn't be alone nights. Especially since you think he knows you suspect him. Why don't you go and visit the Smiths for a week?"

"All right," Cherry agreed, for she didn't really relish the idea of sleeping alone in the little room behind the clinic. In another week, if none of the "boarding school" children developed any whooping cough symptoms, Bertha would move back. "But what worries me," she went on, "is that Spofford may find the money and leave before you have time to check with the philanthropist he'll say he's representing. He has seven nights to dig in, between now and your next visit."

"That would worry me too," Dr. Jessup said, smiling, "*if* I were as sure as you are that the money is buried in the old tobacco field."

Cherry sighed. "There's only one way to prove that it isn't there and that is to get the Clarke and the Smith men to plow that field."

He nodded. "Which means calling a truce. And that I think I can wangle once I can prove to both families that it was Spofford who made the old feud flare up. But my hands are tied until I can be absolutely sure that he's here under false pretenses."

"I know you're right," Cherry said meekly. "And, as Bertha says, my career will probably end someday with a libel suit. But—"

"I'm not so worried," he interrupted, grinning, "about your career being cut short that way. What really worries me is that your impulsiveness may lead you into a dangerous situation. I know you promised Jerry, our minstrel, that you wouldn't do anything foolish, but I want you to make me the same promise. If you're called out at night for any reason, I don't want you to go alone. Linc Smith would be only too glad to go with you."

"I know," Cherry said. "They're all such nice people! Oh, why did that old feud have to flare up before the wedding? If Spofford had only delayed his visit another month, Eliza and Bruce would already have been married!"

Dr. Jessup shrugged. "Spofford obviously rode in as soon as the roads were passable. Which reminds me. The state rural road program now in operation will soon provide transportation by bus for pupils of high school age. The new highway will mean that our hollow will no longer be shut off from the rest of the county." He sighed. "It won't be long before there'll be no need for me and my helicopter. I'll confess that I've always dreamed of someday giving up my practice in Titusville and devoting all my time to a small hospital in a place like this."

"If the Clarke-Smith money is found," Cherry said, "your dream will come true. Bertha feels sure that both families would donate it to the community. And now that the teacher's salary has been taken care of, don't you think they'd want to enlarge the clinic into a small hospital?"

"I do," he agreed. "Lu's mother was terribly impressed with the Titusville Hospital. I took her on a tour and I was really surprised by all the intelligent questions she asked. If you ask me, I think that the reign of the grannies has just about come to an end. Young Mrs. Powell started the new trend, and Lu's successful appendectomy, plus your work with the babies' mothers, has accomplished more than we fully realize now."

"I'll go one step further," Cherry said. "I think Granny Smith is much more modern-minded than she lets on."

"What do you mean by that enigmatic statement?" he asked.

"I don't know exactly," Cherry admitted. "But I keep on getting the impression that she isn't as afraid of the devil as she would like me to believe. She pretended to be badly frightened by that apparition we saw hovering in mid-air between the Carters' lean-to and barn, but I don't think she was. If she had been really terrified she would have hid her head under the covers instead of scurrying out to the yard as fast as she could."

"That's right," Dr. Jessup agreed.

"And," Cherry went on, "I can't take her seriously when she says the devil put a curse on that money and she hopes he'll take it out of here. As you know, Granny

Smith has a very healthy respect for money. I doubt if she'd let even Satan himself leave here with a penny that rightfully belonged to her family. What I'm leading up to is this. If you could make Josh Clarke agree to a truce long enough for all four men to plow the field, I think Granny Smith would see to it that her grandson and great-grandson co-operated. And if the money was found, she'd be the first to suggest that it be used for the building of a small hospital."

Dr. Jessup chuckled. "You obviously know her a lot better than I do. When she and I last discussed medicine, she almost convinced me that her famous garlic grease was the perfect cure for whooping cough. One teaspoonful four times a day, instead of chloromycetin capsules, was her perscription for Billy Carter."

"I know," Cherry said. "She did try to give Billy a teaspoonful of her garlic remedy, but he flatly refused to take it. That's why she left in a huff. I'm sure that right after she left, Mr. Spofford sneaked in and put the basketball under Billy's bed. From his room, Spofford could have seen her leave, and he could also have seen the Carters working down in their field. For the first and only time since he's been staying with the Clarkes, he left by the back door that morning. Of course, when he leaves at night after everyone is asleep, he goes out the back door in order to avoid disturbing anyone. I heard him myself last night and was awfully tempted to follow him."

"Keep right on resisting that temptation," Dr. Jessup said sternly. "I'll feel much better when you're at the Smiths' where you won't be able to hear his nightly departures." They stopped in the Clarkes' front yard, and Dr. Jessup continued: "Move right now, and stay with the Smiths until next Saturday. Granny Smith will be delighted to have you. By that time I'll have checked up on Spofford. If he's a crook, he won't wait here until my next visit. He wouldn't dare."

"That's true," Cherry agreed. "But before you leave, you will talk to Josh Clarke, won't you? If he refuses to agree to a truce, couldn't you drop a hint that it might be a good idea for him to sleep with one eye open? Last Saturday I thought he almost shared my suspicions of his house guest, but obviously he doesn't. If he did he'd have made it a point to stay awake and would have heard the same stealthy sounds I heard last night. Oh, if only we could tell Josh that Jerry feels pretty sure Spofford is Spud Chaseman."

Dr. Jessup sighed. "Without proof, the only hint I can drop to Josh is that I think it would be a good idea for him and the Smiths to plow that field." He stared down at the rolling land that lay between the two hillside homes. "If one man tried to dig up those twenty acres by hand," he said, "it would be like looking for a needle in a haystack. Even if I can't arrange a truce today, I doubt if Spofford will have any luck during the next few nights."

Just then Chase Spofford himself appeared on the porch. "Hello, Jessup," he said cordially, and came down the steps to shake hands with the doctor.

Cherry left them and went inside to pack her week-end bag. In a few minutes Dr. Jessup joined her in the living room. Granny Clarke was on the back porch, starting a new hooked rug. The other members of the family were down in the garden.

"Spofford," Dr. Jessup said quietly, "says he is representing a very rich man who, I happen to know, has suffered from rheumatoid arthritis most of his life." He opened his bag and took out a small instrument on which were printed the words, "Beau Alarm." Pointing to a little button on the side, he said, "With a flick of your thumb you can set off this portable burglar alarm, and the siren will keep on shrieking until it runs down. I always carry it in my bag because I'm often called out at night to some pretty tough neighborhoods in Titusville. From now on until next Saturday, I want you to keep it with you, day and night."

He looked so serious that Cherry instinctively shivered. "I don't need that little bodyguard," she said in what she hoped was a brave voice. "I'm not going to wander around alone at night."

He smiled briefly. "I don't trust you, and I don't trust Spofford. That man's right hand is badly blistered. The instant he shook hands with me he knew he had made a mistake. A little too hastily, and with an angry glance in your direction, he explained the blisters by saying that he'd been helping his host spade up the vegetable garden, which, according to you, was completely planted a week ago."

"That's right," Cherry said, with a sniff. "Spofford has never lifted a finger to help anyone with anything since he arrived."

Dr. Jessup nodded. "I believe you. Furthermore, I strongly suspect that he carries a pistol in a shoulder holster. I saw a bulge under his vest while we were talking. He undoubtedly carries it with him whenever he leaves his room, for fear Eliza might find it while tidying up." He pointed a stern finger at Cherry. "Keep that Beau Alarm on your bed table at night. I'm going to put in a long-distance call to his philanthropist the minute I get back to Titusville."

CHAPTER XIV

A Compromise

CHERRY DID NOT OPEN HER AIR-MAIL LETTERS UNTIL after Dr. Jessup had departed. Too late, she remembered that the package he had brought her was still in the helicopter.

"I wonder who it was from and what was in it," she thought as she settled down on the Smiths' front porch in the late afternoon sunlight. Then she dismissed it from her mind as she hungrily read and reread the letter from her mother.

"We are all well," Mrs. Ames wrote, "although I'm afraid Dr. Joe is working too hard in the new Group Practice Clinic. They're terribly short of nurses, and I really think that as soon as Bertha can spare you, you ought to come home. I don't need to tell you how much it would mean to your father and me, darling, and I'm sure you'd enjoy the work."

Cherry knew she would enjoy the work and the

thought of having a job in Hilton and living at home filled her with nostalgia. The other letter was from Charlie, who wrote:

"Whatever you do, Sis, don't fall in love with a Kentucky mountaineer and stay in Heartbreak Hollow. I'm counting on your spending this summer at home. I applied for and got a counselor job at the YMCA boys' camp. If you work at the new clinic and get the same days off that I do, we could have grand times together. I know just about every town in the whole USA is suffering from the nurse shortage, but charity begins at home, honey."

"It certainly does," Cherry decided. She promptly wrote her mother a long letter, saying that if Dr. Joe and Hilton really needed her she would come home as soon as possible. Then she began a lengthy epistle to Mai Lee.

"Dr. Jessup," she wrote, "is sending you a telegram from Titusville this evening, accepting the prices on your list. It's all too good to be true! I'm enclosing an inventory of the rugs, scarfs, blankets, etc., which we'll send off on the mule train to be shipped direct to Simpson and Company by railway express. They should arrive before the middle of May.

"As Dr. Jessup requested in his wire, all checks should be made payable to him. He was voted the community's banker at a meeting here this afternoon. I hope Miss Righter's check arrives in time for him to bring in some money on his next visit. The people here will have a wonderful time with their 'wish books,' mail-order catalogues to you. They need so many things, Mai Lee, that other people take for granted!

"I'll write as much as I can every day about Heartbreak Hollow, and will take pictures with Bertha's camera. She says that our wandering minstrel took some wonderful color shots last summer. I'm going to send him a message by the mule train asking him to send you a set.

"I'm glad you have three such swell roommates sharing No. 9 with you. Tell that gal who's occupying the room Gwen and I used to share that she can keep it for several more months at least. As soon as Bertha can spare me, I'm going home. Dr. Joe and Hilton need me, Mai Lee. Isn't that wonderful? I can work at the new clinic and live at home!"

Cherry slipped the first pages of what was later to be termed "The Saga of Heartbreak Hollow" into her writing case. Mrs. Bella Smith was blowing on the gourd horn to call the men to supper. Cherry was too tired to eat, but she knew she would have to sit down at the table and try to swallow something. Otherwise, she might hurt the feelings of these kind, hospitable people.

Bruce and his father came out on the porch to scrub their hands and faces at the "washing bench." Cherry thought that Bruce looked almost as ill as Eliza did, and her heart ached with sympathy for them both.

After they had sat for a minute with bowed heads as Lincoln Smith said grace, Granny exploded the bomb shell. "Tomorrer," she announced, "the old tobaccer field is a-goen to be plowed up. Fust thing in the mornen."

Bella Smith dropped a serving spoon with a loud clatter. Her husband's usually stolid face was filled with amazement.

"I don't aim to listen to no arggyments from you, Linc," Granny told him firmly. "You an' Bruce kin plow one half, an' the Clarkes, t'other. 'Tain't no need fer you-all to speak one to t'other whilst you is a-worken. But Debby an' me has come to the conclusion that the missen money might be buried out thar. If so, hit will turn up tomorrer; if not, no harm has been done."

"But Josh—" Lincoln Smith began.

"Josh Clarke an' Malcolm is agreeable," his grandmother told him. "The doctor-man tole me so hisself jist afore he tuck off in his flyen contraption."

Cherry stared at her. Dr. Jessup was indeed a wonder! He had somehow managed to make time for a visit to both families before his departure. She was glad now that she had told him she felt sure he could count on Granny Smith's co-operation if he proposed a truce.

It was not, of course, going to be a truce in the real sense of the word, but it would accomplish one thing. The field would be plowed, and by dusk tomorrow everyone in the hollow would know whether or not the money had been buried there.

"Tomorrer is the Sabbath," Granny Smith was saying, "an' iffen you-all was to plow with the idee of planten, hit wouldn't be fitten. But sence you ain't aimen to plant, hit *is* fitten."

"Oh," Cherry cried excitedly, "I do hope you find the money tomorrow."

Lincoln Smith shrugged. "Iffen hit's thar we-all will find hit."

But they didn't find it. The four men worked from dawn to dusk, refusing to stop even for a bite of lunch, and by the time the sun had disappeared behind Old Desolate, they had turned up every foot of the land. It was twilight when Bruce and his father returned to their home, looking tired and discouraged.

"Someone," Lincoln Smith said dourly, "had been a-diggen out thar afore us'n. I reckon whoever hit was found the money—iffen it was thar."

To Cherry's surprise, Granny Smith did not look at all depressed. "So you didn't see no sign o' a big iron caldron?" she asked cheerfully. "An' you kep' an eye on the Clarkes to make shore they didn't come acrost hit?"

"Caldron?" Cherry repeated. "The other day you said something about a barrel. Do you think now that the money was buried in a caldron, Granny?"

"I'm shore hit was, chile," she said, smiling mysteriously. "I ricollect now how them gold pieces shone in the moonlight when old Lazarus was a-pouren them out o' his saddlebags into hit."

Cherry glanced at her sharply. Granny Smith, she decided, remembered a lot more about the era when the feud began than she had been letting on.

She beckoned Cherry into her bedroom and whispered, chuckling, "Did you happen to examinate that city feller's face whilst the men was a-plowen?"

Cherry nodded. She had even taken a candid-camera shot of Mr. Spofford, who looked apoplectic with rage most of the day. "We both knew he was the one who was digging," Cherry said. "And he certainly didn't act as though he had already found the money."

"He didn't find hit," the little old lady cackled. " 'Cause hit wan't never in the tobaccer field. Lordy, hit does my heart good to ponder on how he lost sleep nights a-diggen, an' a-diggen, all to no purpose!"

"Why, Granny," Cherry cried, "you sound as though you know where it is."

"The onliest thing I know fer sartain," she said, "is that the city feller hain't the devil like I suspicioned at fust. Why, he hain't nothen but a no-count furriner!"

"That's right," Cherry agreed. "And maybe he'll go away now that there's no point in digging any more."

"I bin figgeren on that," Granny Smith said. "Most likely he's already cotched his nag an' is saddlen up right now."

"I wouldn't be at all surprised," Cherry said. "Even though the moon is waning, it still shines brightly enough for him to follow the road up and over the mountain. And he's used to staying awake nights, so there's no danger of his falling asleep in the saddle." She sighed with relief. "I think perhaps we've seen the last of him."

"He desarves punishment for spilen our wool an'

pizenin' the Clarkes' hog," Granny Smith said bitterly. "But I reckon the good Lord will take keer o' him in time."

"Oh," Cherry gasped. "Then you don't think it was the devil who played all those mean tricks on you and the Clarkes?"

"Hit was that city feller, jist like you said, Cherry. Do you ricollect the night atter the rain when you an' me seed that face up at Carters'?"

Cherry nodded. "If only Mr. Carter had looked in the loft I'm sure he would have found Mr. Spofford hiding there."

"He shore would. 'Cause I watched from my window fer quite a spell. An' atter he had made sure the folks was asleep, he come out an' tuck off down the hill like a fox with the hound-dogs atter him. I seed him jist as plain, but I didn't say nothen to nobody." She tossed her head. "I don't aim to have Zeke Carter laugh at me but oncet. But I knowed then that the city feller wan't Satan. He was powerful a-feerd when he tuck off down the hill, Cherry, an' Satan, he ain't scairt o' ary a pussen."

"I guess Mr. Spofford had a bad moment when he heard me begging Mr. Carter to search the loft," Cherry said, with a laugh. "I only wish Ezekiel had been watching at the window too, and had seen that man sneak out of his barn."

Granny Smith nodded. "Atter that, I kep' an eye on the field nights, but he didn't do no diggen whilst the minstrel was hyar." She abruptly changed the subject, and patted Cherry's hand, smiling. "Garlic grease rubbed on j'ints achen with rheumatiz is mighty holpful. But I didn't give none to Deb. Tole her take them leetle white pilts o' yourn, sence hit 'pears like they didn't give Lu the fits. Reckon Debby wouldn't o' bin playen on her dulcimer all week iffen hit hadn't bin fer you."

"I'm awfully glad," Cherry said gratefully, "that you persuaded Mrs. Clarke to take the aspirin Dr. Jessup prescribed."

"We got to hev a bigger clinic," the old woman continued, "so's we-all kin hev pilts like them handy. An' a place where a body kin go when he gits real bad sick like Lu. Deb an' me is gitten on in yars." She chuckled mysteriously. "Iffen I should happenchance to come acrost thet money, I'd say the doctor-man should hev hit, I would!"

CHAPTER XV

Adventure at Midnight

A COLD WIND DESCENDED ON THE HOLLOW THAT NIGHT and shook the big frame house in its teeth. It rattled the windows, roared down the chimneys, and even the wide floor boards creaked in protest. Cherry slept fitfully. The moon, a platinum crescent now, shone right in her window, making the room as bright as though the lanterns were burning.

Shivering in spite of her warm flannel pajamas, Cherry snuggled under the mound of coverlets, and dozed. A few minutes before midnight she awoke to find herself sitting bolt upright in bed. She never knew what sound had startled her out of her dream, but her subconscious mind told her that it had come from Granny Smith's room.

Cherry was out of bed in a flash. The old lady might be having a severe attack of asthma. She might be having so much difficulty in breathing that she could not cry out for help.

Cherry slid her feet into warm slippers and pulled her coat around her shoulders. There was no point in awakening the little old lady if she were sleeping peacefully, but Cherry felt that the sound which had awakened *her* should be investigated. She tiptoed out into the living room and opened the door to Granny Smith's room a crack. The bed was empty. She opened the door wider. Granny was not in her room. And then through the gleaming windowpanes Cherry saw her.

The little old woman, wearing her sunbonnet and shawl, was trudging determinedly down the slope toward the tobacco field. For a moment Cherry was too surprised to move. Then the thought occurred to her that Granny might be sleepwalking. Somnambulists, she knew, were apt to stumble and hurt themselves if rudely awakened. The wise thing to do was to follow her quickly, but quietly, and gently lead her back to the house.

Cherry slipped her arms into the sleeves of her coat and silently left the house by the back door. At first she tried to run but soon realized that running downhill on rough ground in flapping bedroom slippers was impossible. She couldn't even walk very fast, not nearly as fast as Granny, who was trotting sure-footedly along, every minute widening the distance between her and Cherry.

She skirted the newly plowed land and started up toward the rocky ridge that bounded the field on the west. Cherry followed, hurrying as fast as she could. If the ground had not been so rough and the night so cold she would have kicked off the warm slippers that were holding her back. She thrust her cold hands into her coat pockets and then her fingers touched the little Beau Alarm. Guiltily she remembered that she had promised to keep it on the table beside her bed at night, but had left it in the pocket where she had put it earlier in the evening.

"Well, anyway," she reflected, "I'm obeying Dr. Jessup's orders now, even if it is an accident that I happen to have my bodyguard with me at the moment."

Belatedly she remembered that one of his strictest orders had been that she was not to leave the house at night unless accompanied by Bruce or Lincoln Smith. "The patient always comes first," she told the voice of her conscience. "Besides, there's nothing to be afraid of now that Mr. Spofford is probably many miles away."

She made better time as the ground began to slope gently up toward the rocky hill. Where was Granny Smith's dream leading her? Surely, even in her sleep, she must be aware enough to avoid the hill. But she kept steadily on. Cherry was really worried now. It would be better to shout and rudely awaken the little old lady than to risk letting her attempt to climb up those treacherous-looking rocks.

"Granny," she called. "Granny Smith." But the wind, blowing from the west, carried her voice away in the wrong direction. Cherry kicked off her slippers and began to run. The cold, jagged stones cut and bruised her bare feet, but she ran on until she tripped and fell.

sprawling headlong in the freshly plowed earth. Stunned and breathless, Cherry lay there for a moment, hopelessly watching Granny Smith, who had now stopped at the foot of the rocks. She was too far away for Cherry to see what she was doing, but she seemed to be searching for something.

And then, from the corner of one eye, Cherry saw someone come out of the woods that bounded the field on the Clarke side. "It must be Josh," Cherry decided, scrambling to her feet. "He probably heard me calling Granny although she couldn't."

The man began to run toward the old woman, who, at the same moment, began to clamber up the rocks. She climbed as agilely as a cat but Cherry stood watching her, frozen with fright. If she were suddenly awakened now she would certainly fall and hurt herself badly.

Cherry forced her sore feet to carry her onward over the rough ground. She could see the profile of the man who had run out of the woods now and knew that it was not Josh. The man was smooth-shaven and carried a pistol in one hand.

So Spofford had not galloped away after all!

The gun's barrel gleamed in the silvery moonlight, and Cherry, staring at it with horror, stumbled again. When she weakly staggered to her feet, there was no sign of Granny Smith, and Spofford was standing at the foot of the hill, gazing upward. Cherry was still so far away that she could not see the expression on his face, but she guessed that it showed both triumph and greed.

For she realized now that Granny Smith had not been walking in her sleep. In her tomboy days, Martha Smith must have discovered a cave among those rocks and had forgotten about it until that very evening. While the men plowed the field, she had probably been living in the past, recalling long-forgotten childhood events. That explained why she had not been depressed when they did not find the caldron. She must have made up her mind to search the cave by moonlight. If only she could have waited until morning!

Spofford, Cherry saw, was wearing riding boots. He had probably been in the Clarkes' stable stealthily saddling his horse when the wind brought him her cries of "Granny. Granny Smith." From the opposite hill he could have plainly seen the little old woman hurrying toward the rocky ridge, and must have decided to follow her, taking the short cut through the Clarke woods.

If Granny Smith came out of the cave with a caldron full of gold, he would make her hand it over to him. There was nothing Cherry could do to stop him. Screaming was a waste of breath. She had already yelled herself hoarse and nobody except Spofford had heard her. There was no time in which to run back to the Smiths' for help. By the time she climbed the slope, he would be on his horse, galloping away with the money. And there was no point in running toward that gun.

But run toward it Cherry did, for she could not bear the thought of the frail, elderly woman facing that man and his pistol alone. Even if she didn't reappear on the rocky ridge with the money he might handle her roughly out of pure spite. Cherry remembered with a shudder the barely suppressed anger on his face when she had taken a candid-camera shot of him while the four men were plowing the field.

A hard clump of overturned sod tripped her and she lurched to her knees, almost sobbing with exhaustion. Tears of pain and discouragement filmed her eyes. She clenched her fists and tried to rub them away, forgetting that her hands were caked with mud. Momentarily blinded now, she groped through her coat pockets for a handkerchief. And then her fingers touched the Beau Alarm.

The scream of the siren shut out all other sounds, and by the time Cherry could see clearly again, Granny Smith had climbed down to the foot of the hill. She and Spofford were standing like statues, staring in Cherry's direction, and pouring from the rocks above them was a black cloud.

To Cherry's surprise, Granny Smith suddenly threw herself on the ground to lie motionless. Simultaneously, Spofford turned and ran back toward the woods. As the wail of the siren died away, the sinister cloud flowed down from the rocks like dark molasses. From it came a deep angry roar that filled Cherry's heart with a new terror.

Bees! Wild bees! Thousands of them in an endlessly swirling and swooping mass pursued Spofford as he ran, shrieking and waving his arms.

"The spring," Cherry yelled, hoping the wind would carry her voice to him. "Head for the spring and stay underwater."

Men, women, and children were converging on the tobacco field from all directions. Cherry hesitated long enough to make sure that the maddened swarm of bees were completely ignoring Granny Smith's still body. Then she raced back toward the Smiths', thinking:

"Bees loathe the smell of garlic! Shrewd Granny must have coated her face and hands with garlic grease before leaving the house. As long as she lies perfectly still, the bees won't bother her. They're going to wreak their vengeance on Spofford with his sweet-smelling hair pomade. *They may kill or blind him!*"

Forgotten were Cherry's bleeding feet and bruised knees. A man's life was at stake. Tarring and feathering was a mild punishment compared to that which the bees were meting out. His heavy jacket, riding breeches, and boots would protect most of his body. But his face! His eyes, ears, and nose would swell out of all proportion, and, most dangerous of all, his throat might close. As soon as he could be rescued he should be given ice to suck. But there was no ice.

"If he headed for the spring, as anyone in his right mind would," Cherry decided, "he'll involuntarily drink a lot of that icy water, which should help to reduce the swelling in his neck."

If he could still swallow by the time she reached him with her bag, several pyribenzamine tablets would be in order. Then hot poultices of sodium bicarbonate. After that, the stings must be carefully removed, one by one, and the wounds painted with tincture of iodine. He would, furthermore, almost certainly be chilled when he was dragged out of the spring, and suffering from shock.

Suddenly the responsibility seemed too much for Cherry. She wished with all her heart that Granny Smith could share it with her. If the old woman insisted upon using hot onion poultices, Cherry would not object. Anything, anything at all to keep the man's throat from closing.

She looked up to see Bruce and his father riding down the slope astride mules.

"The spring," she shouted to them hoarsely. "The spring. Mr. Spofford. Bees, thousands of them. You must do something to force them back to the rocks."

Lincoln pointed to the smoke that was rising above the Clarkes' woods and said calmly, "Smudge. Reckon Josh an' Malcolm got that fyer a-goen soon as they seed what we seed when that onairthly noise woke us."

They galloped across the field, their mules' hoofs splattering clods of earth in all directions. Then Cherry saw Bella Smith riding toward her on one mule and leading another.

"I got your doctoren poke," she said. "Git up on Jenny. She's a hinny an' mighty sure-footed an' gentle."

Cherry had never been on a horse and had never thought that one moonlight night she would ride a mule bareback across a freshly plowed field. But she was so tired and her feet were so sore that she didn't hesitate a minute. As she told Bertha later, "I didn't mount Jenny in the orthodox fashion. I simply flopped on with a grateful sigh."

In a few minutes they could see the crowd that had gathered around the smudge fire on the windward side of the spring. The spiraling black smoke from it cut off their view of the bee horde, and Cherry knew that Spofford could soon be rescued.

It was Josh Clarke, with Lincoln Smith's help, who dragged him from the spring. His face was swollen beyond recognition, and he was only semiconscious. For too many minutes he had had to choose between being stung to death or drowning.

"I don't like to see even a rat git drownded," Linc said to Josh as they laid him on the blanket Eliza quickly spread out beside the spring. "But 'twas him who pizened your hog, Josh, an' spiled my wool."

As Cherry slid from Jenny's back and groped for the man's pulse, she heard Josh reply:

"I suspicioned hit, Linc. Cherry, thar, done as good as tole me, but I didn't aim to say nothen to you' less you spoke fust."

"Hit was a good thing you started that smudge so quick," Lincoln said succinctly, but his voice was full of approval and friendliness.

Spofford's pulse was weak, but since he was still breathing, there was no need for artificial respiration.

Cherry looked up at the two men. "We've got to take him to the nearest house where he can be dried and warmed. Then I'll need lots of hot water for poultices." As she spoke she quickly made an improvised stretcher by rolling the edges of the blanket in toward Spofford.

The men caught on quickly and soon, with three of them on each side, they were carrying the too-quiet patient up the road to the Clarkes', where Lu and the granny already had a fire blazing.

Granny Clarke timidly handed Cherry a bottle of ammonia. "Hit's mighty good fer bee bites," she said.

Cherry managed a grateful smile as she uncorked the bottle and held it under Spofford's swollen nose. In a few seconds his puffy eyelids fluttered and he began to moan. As she waited for the big pot of water to heat she moistened bandages with ammonia and laid them on his neck, chin, and cheeks.

"Be careful of his eyes." It was Bertha's voice, sounding very far away. "Here, honey, let me put this paste of sodium bicarb on the lids."

Later Cherry realized dazedly as she worked that Granny Smith was there helping, too, and that Linc and Josh, when they undressed Spofford and wrapped him in heated blankets, had discussed and cleared up every angle of the events which had caused the feud to flare up.

Dawn was pinking the sky above Old Desolate before Cherry felt she could leave her patient in the capable hands of Bertha and the two grannies. His throat was not going to close, his loud groans of agony gave every indication that he was now very much alive.

Then, unaccountably, Jerry was there, saying, "I got to worrying for fear you wouldn't keep your promise. And so did Dad when I told him about you and how Spofford uses the same pomade that Spud Chaseman used. I brought him along so he could positively identify that crook."

Cherry laughed, almost hysterical with weariness. "Your father couldn't identify him now. No one could. His face is nothing—nothing but lumps."

"Hit don't make no difference," Bella Smith said as she and Jerry gently led Cherry into Granny Clarke's room. Eliza and Bruce, arm in arm, followed.

"That's right," Jerry said. "Dad's here for the wedding, which is the most important thing."

Cherry collapsed on the edge of the big four-poster bed. "Is it true, Eliza?" she asked. "Are you and Bruce going to be married tomorrow—today?"

Eliza nodded, half smiling, half crying with happiness. "Granny Smith, she found the money. Hit was in the bee cave. Ary a soul dairst look thar fer hit. 'Twan't safe, 'cepten at night an' all kivered with garlic grease. Hit wan't never in no holler tree. My great-grandpappy thought hit was 'cause the onliest words his paw said to him afore he died was, 'Foller the bees.' "

Bruce spoke up then. "My granny didn't know about that till t'other day when Eliza's granny tole her. An' iffen you hadn't got them two speaken one to t'other, Cherry, the money, hit wouldn't niver hev bin found."

Granny Smith herself bustled into the room then. "Hit's the truth," she said, "An' hit hain't likely the bee cave would o' come to my mind whilst the men was a-plowen the field iffen Miss Cherry hadn't kep' talken erbout putten bees in a pussen's bonnet. Now, Eliza an' Bruce, you'd better go. The pore chile needs sleep."

A few seconds later from far off came the sound of something that sounded as though the bees might have begun to swarm again. But Cherry was too tired to care. Mingling with the roar was Granny Smith's old voice as she suddenly leaned down to lay her withered cheek on Cherry's:

"I declare, chile," she whispered, firmly tucking a mound of covers around Cherry, "you is a mighty knowen young'un!"

Cherry knew she was dreaming when she heard Granny Clarke add in a voice loud enough to drown out the sound of the helicopter's rotor blades, "She shorely is, Marthy. I reckon that's the doctor-man a-comen to fotch that varmint."

CHAPTER XVI

"Weep No More"

"BUT, CHERRY," MIDGE WAILED, "THAT ISN'T THE END of the story. You haven't answered half of my questions."

Cherry stared out her bedroom window at the apple blossoms. "Kentucky is beautiful in April," she said, "but there's no place like Hilton in May."

Midge bounced up and down on the bed impatiently. "Answer me, yes or no, are you or are you not in love with (a) Jerry, the Minstrel; (b) Frank Jessup?"

"*Dr.* Frank Jessup to you, imp," Cherry said fondly to her young neighbor. "And the answer to both questions is, no. But I *am* in love with Happy, alias *Heartbreak,* Hollow. I'm going back there someday, but when I do everything will be so changed I probably won't like it. The new road, the hospital, the beautiful nurse-and-teacher's modern residence, buses taking the older children back and forth to and from high school, trucks coming in regularly with mail and supplies." She sighed. "No, on second thought, I guess I won't go back."

"Question two," Midge went on, counting on her slim fingers. "Was Mr. Spofford representing a rich philanthropist, or wasn't he?"

"I refuse to answer any more questions," Cherry said. "You don't know how tired I am, Midge. I flew to New York right after the wedding. That meant a trip by helicopter and a longer one by bus before I even reached Louisville. Then, all the time I was packing my trunk at No. 9, I was being interviewed by Miss Jane Righter, and the men from Simpson's publicity department. After that I took a plane to Chicago. Now at last I'm home, and I may have to go on duty at the new GMP clinic tomorrow." She yawned, her brown eyes teasing. "Can't you wait until next fall and read the story in the newspapers and magazines?"

Midge threw a pillow at her. Cherry tossed it back. "Okay, fiend. Mr. Spud Chaseman was not representing anyone. That was one reason why he planned to leave the hollow the night after the Clarke-Smith land was plowed. He knew Dr. Jessup was going to check up on him, and since the money obviously wasn't buried in the field, he came to the same conclusion that everyone else reached years ago."

Midge nodded. "That the money was destroyed during the fire when the feud began. But, Cherry, the fire would only have melted the gold pieces. Why didn't someone look for a nice chunk or nugget which could have been turned in to the United States Mint?"

"They did look for it," Cherry said, "but they didn't look in the right place. The Smiths searched every inch of their property and so did the Clarkes. Even if the feud had ended two generations ago, and they had plowed and planted the tobacco field, they wouldn't have found it. Because no one ever went near the bee cave. It took Granny Smith to realize that Lazarus Clarke hid the money at night when it would have been safe to hide the caldron among the rocks on the ridge."

"*If* he rubbed himself with garlic first," Midge added, giggling. "I know you were terribly worried for fear those bees would kill old Spud Spofford, but I think it was a good joke on him. He had no business following Granny Smith that night with a pistol. I suppose when he looked down from the Clarkes' barn and saw her heading for the cliffs he realized for the first time that the money might have been hidden there."

"That's right," Cherry said. "Although he did his digging at night when the bees were quiet, he dug at the other end of the field, for he was as sure as I was that Lazarus Clarke and Dolph Smith had buried the money somewhere near one of the two homes. Those men were smart. They couldn't have picked a safer place. Most wild bees do build their hives in hollow trees, and although Lazarus' son must have known about the bee cave in the rocks, you can't blame him for not searching there." She shuddered reminiscently. "Honestly, Midge, if you had seen that black cloud and heard the roar! It was absolutely terrifying! I don't know how Granny Smith had the nerve to do what she did. And, actually, you know, it was Spofford who saved her from being badly stung. Her garlic grease wouldn't have kept these maddened bees away for long. If they hadn't been attracted by Spofford's hair pomade they would have descended on her in a mass."

Midge grinned. "The fact that he ran and she lay quietly on the ground helped. I suppose old Lazarus planned to smoke the bees out when he went back for the money. I wonder why he wasn't stung when he put it in the cave."

"He probably was," Cherry said. "But he raised bees and sold the honey for his 'pay money' until he decided to pool his resources with the Smiths. Old bee farmers generally develop a tolerance to formic acid, which is the fluid bees inject when they sting you."

"One more question," Midge said. "How come Eliza got married that very morning? She didn't have a new pair of shoes."

"I'll have to go back to Dr. Jessup to explain that," Cherry said. "After he left the hollow Saturday night he put in a long-distance call to the philanthropist, who was away for the weekend. He finally tracked him down somewhere on Long Island late Sunday night. When he learned that the philanthropist had never even heard of Spofford, Frank began to worry. He was worried enough when he left or he wouldn't have given me the Beau Alarm, but then he realized that Spofford, knowing he was going to check up on him, might do something desperate. So he hopped in his helicopter and flew back, arriving just in time to bring Eliza a new pair of shoes."

Midge sniffed with disgust. "Now you're kidding. He couldn't have known her size, for one thing, and he also had no idea that Jerry's father was there or that the feud had ended."

Cherry laughed. "No, he didn't, but in his helicopter was a package for me from home. When I opened it I found a pretty pair of red ballet slippers and in one toe was a note from Dad saying, 'Rubber heels are no good for square dancing.' Dad and I have always had a joke about red shoes ever since he first read me the fairy story about the vain little girl whose little red shoes almost danced her into the grave. The girl's name was Karen, and it's one of Andersen's fairy tales. I know it by heart, because when I was a little girl I was always crazy about red shoes and used to pretend mine were magic."

"But you weren't vain, Cherry," Midge said, giving her an affectionate hug. "In fact, you're too darned modest. If I were going to relate the saga of Heartbreak Hollow I'd tell it quite differently."

Cherry settled back against the pillows. "You tell it," she said, laughing.

"I will," Midge replied, "and don't forget my name is Cherry. Well, once upon a time I went to a place where everyone was poor and unhappy because a mean old ogre had recently come there. He had taken all the people's gold and had cast a spell on the princess so she no longer loved the prince. I donned my coat of mail, mounted my white charger, and, with my trusty sword at my side, rode right up to the ogre and bravely chopped off his head. And they all lived happily ever after."

Cherry shook with laughter. "The only riding I did was on a gray mule and I was wearing very muddy flannel pajamas."

"Speaking of pajamas," Midge interrupted, "did anyone ever find Zeke Carter's red flannels?"

"Malcolm Clarke did," Cherry told her. "When he was plowing his end of the field, he found a box buried there. In it were the flannels, the neckties Spofford accused Billy of stealing, and a tube of luminescent paint. Malcolm gave the box to his father, who, in turn, wordlessly handed the cache over to the Smiths."

Midge giggled. "That was one way of putting a bee in their bonnets. It's a wonder they didn't tar and feather him then and there. And I guess he wishes they had."

"Those people," Cherry said, "wouldn't tar and feather anyone. You can't imagine how kind and gentle they are. And if the children weren't so obedient, they would have played in that field and have found the box long before Malcolm Clarke did."

"Well," Midge said, "I'm certainly glad the wind carried your voice over to the Clarkes' stable that exciting night. Otherwise, Spofford would have got off scot-free."

"It's an ill wind," Cherry agreed, "that blows no good. If Spofford hadn't come to the hollow the money might never have been found. There wasn't any reason to renew the search for it until he made the feud flare up and caused Eliza and Bruce so much unhappiness. I detested him from the moment he came snooping around the clinic. Although I thought so at first, I soon realized that he hadn't come calling on Bertha and me just to gossip. He came because he wanted to make sure his tricks had been successful and hoped we'd tell him that Eliza had been crying because Bruce refused to speak to her. When I didn't tell him anything of the kind, he listened outside our window until Bruce arrived to tell us his granny had been badly frightened."

"I detest him, too," Midge said. "When he confessed, did he tell you what gave him the idea of masquerading as a devil?"

Cherry sighed. "Granny Clarke did. Shortly after he arrived at the Carters' she saw something, nobody knows exactly what, but she still swears it had a long tail. From his bedroom window he heard her describing the apparition to Mrs. Carter, who, at the very moment, was hanging Ezekiel's red flannels on the line. Later that morning, when he realized he was going to have trouble buying the Clarke-Smith land, he bought the ties from Granny Smith, and in the afternoon he ruined their wool. While he was in the barn he put something in the mules' feedbins which has the same effect on animals that benzedrine has on humans. After that, he poisoned the Clarkes' hog. But just in case the feud didn't flare up right away, he began to dig as soon as it got dark that night, garbed as the devil. When he saw the lights suddenly go on in the Smiths' house, he decided he had better quit until he could be sure everyone in the hollow was sound asleep. So he changed back into city clothes, buried his costume, and came down to the clinic."

"Thus providing himself with an alibi," Midge put in, "in case anyone asked any questions, and at the same time giving him the chance to ask *you* some questions which you were smart enough not to answer."

"I wasn't smart," Cherry corrected her. "I was just plain mad. Granny Smith was the smart one. She detested him and his hair pomade as much as I did, but it was she who led him into the trap which almost finished him."

"She didn't know she was going to trap him," Midge argued mischievously. "And she wouldn't have if it hadn't been for you with your bees and bonnets."

Cherry jumped out of bed. "I don't aim to listen to sech outlandish nonsense. Granny Smith," she said emphatically, "is the real heroine of the saga."

A masculine voice across the hall began to sing:

"Weep no more, my lady,
Weep no more today."

"Charlie," Midge said, "is taking a shower."

"And," Cherry added, "he is putting a finis to my story."

Holding hands, they both joined in the chorus:

"We will sing one song
For my old Kentucky home,
For my old Kentucky home
Far away!"